I0603337

PENINSULA PROMISES

HEATHER REYBURN

Copyright © 2021 by Heather Reyburn

All rights reserved. No part of this publication may be reproduced, distributed or transmitted in any form or by any means, without prior written permission.

This is a work of fiction. Names, characters, places, and incidents are a product of the author's imagination. Locales and public names are sometimes used for atmospheric purposes. Any resemblance to actual people, living or dead, is completely coincidental.

Cover design: Patti Roberts

Heather Reyburn

www.heatherreyburn.com

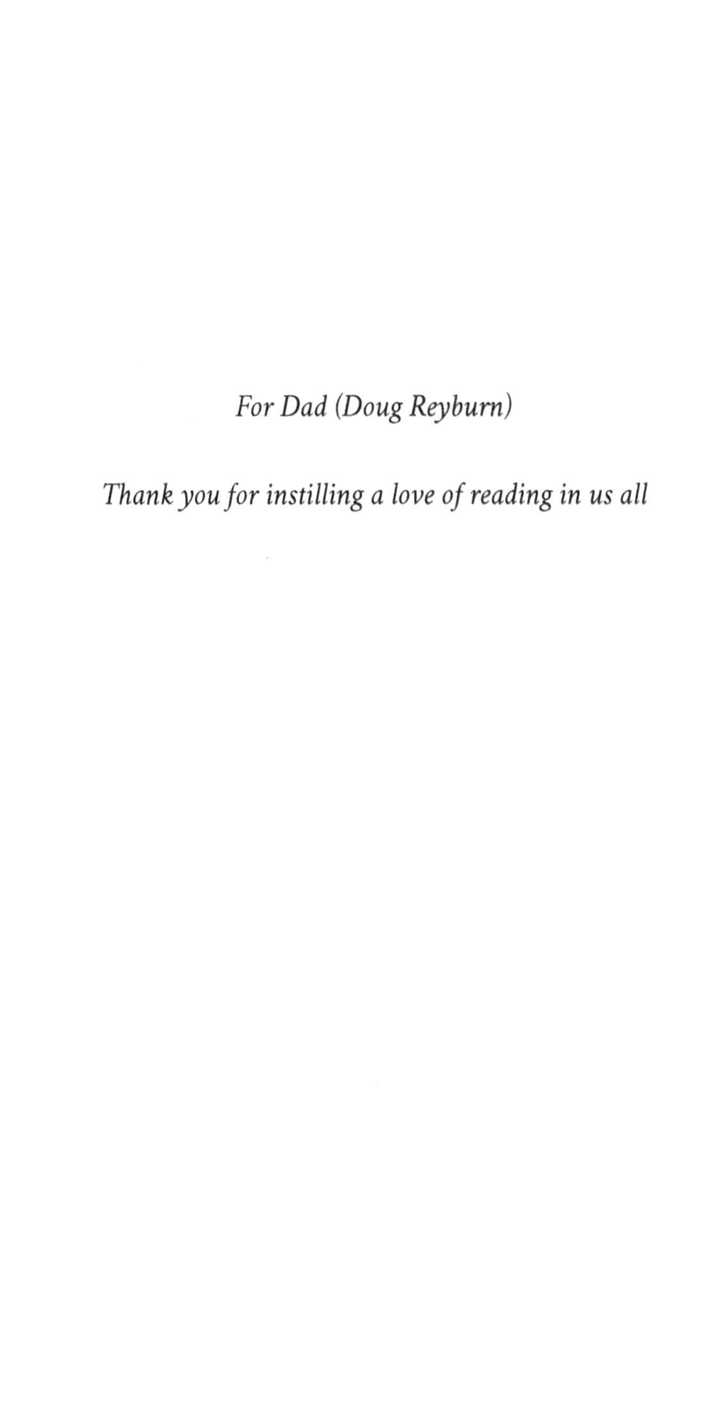

For Dad (Doug Reyburn)

Thank you for instilling a love of reading in us all

PROLOGUE

September 1921

He retched and coughed, regaining consciousness as his stomach ejected a stream of salt water.

After gagging, he swallowed, raised his head, and pushed himself to a sitting position. Sand filled his eyes and nose, and he wiped it away with a clumsy hand shrivelled from long immersion in the sea.

Blinking hard, his vision cleared, and he looked around, a frown deepening across his brow. Black sand surrounded him, and he scooped up a handful, opened his fist and waited for it to trickle through his fingers. Instead, the dark grains clung to his skin like miniature magnets, and he stared at them, mesmerised.

The wind blew off the sea, and in spite of the sun above and a warm surface beneath his feet, a shiver ran down his back. Dropping his head, he searched his clouded memory, his perplexed gaze coming to rest on the ragged pair of trousers and woollen jersey hanging damply on his body.

After struggling to stand he staggered, overcome by a wave of dizziness. He paused, motionless for a few seconds, regained his balance, and stared intently around as though committing these foreign surroundings to memory. On glimpsing a broken lifebuoy laying half-buried a few feet away, he moved closer to stare at the faded letters on the white and red remnant.

H-A-N-N-E.

He squeezed his eyes shut, willing his mind to clear, to offer a hint of recognition.

Nothing.

Who am I?

How did I get here?

He opened his eyes again and gazed unseeing at the piles of driftwood and shells of every size and colour strewn across the wind-swept beach and along the dark foreshore. Seagulls shrieked and swooped above him, as though they too wanted to know why he had intruded into their space.

Fear trickled through his belly, and he stumbled forward, an unexplained urge guiding him inland, over the sand dunes.

I must find fresh water and safety.

Probing his teeth with a thick, furry tongue, he tasted blood. And when the sun disappeared behind a cloud and a squall blew off the ocean, soaking his back, he tried to run, chapped lips stinging as he sucked in deep breaths, sand slipping beneath his bare feet and drawing them downward in a clinging embrace.

On reaching firmer ground, he paused, cringing at the spiky grasses and bracken scratching at his ankles and feet. He looked up, surprised to find himself surrounded by clumps of tall grass, whose feathery, silvery fronds reached skyward and swayed in the wind. In the distance, the parched foliage was met by thick bush.

Something about the trees and deep green ferns triggered a brief vision of another place, another time …

He sagged against a tree trunk, waiting while his laboured breathing eased, and once more studied his surrounds. When exhaustion rose to overwhelm him, he sank gratefully into the bush's soft embrace. On his knees, he crawled into a nest of cushioning moss and damp leaves, covered his face with his hands, and listened.

Above him, raindrops dripped from overhanging fronds and branches, soft plops of falling droplets soothing to his ears. Shuffling into a foetal position, he rested his head on an exposed tree root. Blood pounded in his ears, deadening the sounds of the bush as he scrunched up his face, straining to remember something.

Anything.

He must have drifted off to sleep, for he was woken sometime later by the sun filtering through the leaves overhead. Twittering noises penetrated his consciousness, and he sat up. Flitting around him were two tiny birds, their brown and white bodies flecked with gold and their tails splayed, fan-like. They were like nothing he had ever seen—or could recall.

As though urging him to follow, they wove back and forth, darting away and returning. He obeyed, treading carefully amongst the cool undergrowth. When his hearing caught the faint trickle of water close by, he hurried towards the sound, reassured by the rivulet gushing gently from a bank and spilling over the rocks. He dropped to his knees and drank deeply.

With his burning thirst quenched, he slumped against the bank, grasping at ferns as exhaustion overtook him once more. Shaken and dizzy, he gave in, closed his eyes, and allowed the darkness to claim him.

CHAPTER 1

Karaka, South Auckland, October 1935

Alice Simpson straightened the daffodils in the vase and laid gentle hands on her daughter's grave. "I'm sorry, sweet-pea. I'm not going to be able to visit you as often. Your daddy, brothers, and I are moving to a new district. I wonder what you'd think of that?" She spoke softly, consumed with an ache, an emptiness she could neither soothe nor fill.

Sitting back on her heels, she pulled the cardigan tight around her shoulders. It might be spring, but today a cold wind blew, bringing with it a taste of the sea. Grey clouds scudded overhead, heavy and threatening. She glanced into the wicker basket beside her, studying the cherubic face of her fourth child, dark lashes resting on pink cheeks, the tiny rosebud mouth. John was her special gift, a miniature of Harry, her husband.

Turning back to her daughter's headstone, she whispered, "Bye-bye, little one. You are always in my heart and in my thoughts."

A tear slid down her cheek as she stepped away from the grave, hearing her father's words replaying in her ears. *"Do as your husband bids and go where he goes. You're strong and healthy enough to have more children, so stop your nonsense about a dead baby. Women have lost children since the beginning of time, and you are no different."*

Fury at his bitter words surged again, heightened by what felt like betrayal at the hands of her beloved eldest brother. Showing none of the childhood kindness she remembered, he had sided with their father. Between them, the two men had opened her eyes to how things really were—and would always be.

At the time, she had resolved to compose herself long enough to withdraw from the gloomy formal dining room, where the family gathered once a month after church, and seek Harry out.

On their homeward journey, she had leaned against her husband to whisper, "You're right. It's time we did what we want to do, not what our parents dictate."

Smiling and squeezing her hand, he'd promised, "And we will have a good life."

She tipped her head back as a raindrop splashed on her hat, and another one promptly landed on the tip of her nose. Wiping the drops and tears away, she picked up the baby basket and hurried to the buggy.

"You're a good boy, Duke." She patted the dozing horse before leaning over and placing the baby on the leather bench seat. Fishing out a raincoat from the seat pocket, she gave it a shake before thrusting her arms into the sleeves. When a gust of wind attempted to rip the coat from her, she turned her back to the squall and tied the belt firmly around her waist. Using the cast-iron step, she hauled herself into the buggy and grasped the reins. With the baby basket snug against her side, she clicked the gelding into a brisk walk and turned onto the road.

As the rain increased, pattering on the sparse canvas roof above her head, she urged Duke on, glad as ever of the horse's kind, reliable nature. Recalling her family's horrified reaction when Harry had gifted her the ex-trotter at Christmas, the edges of her lips tipped upward. She had come to love the gelding and quickly adjusted to his two speeds—a sprightly walk or a wild, extended gait, halfway between a trot and a run. Her siblings tut-tutted and neighbours leapt to the roadside whenever she careered past them, one hand on her hat, the other holding the reins in a firm grip, and a broad grin on her face.

On this occasion, she had the road to herself. She bent her head against the driving rain, shielding baby John with the skirt of her coat. Duke remained steadfast in the bad weather, his rhythmic gait devouring the five-mile journey to the small timber farmhouse.

Her home ... but not for much longer.

———

ALICE SCURRIED TOWARDS THE BACK PORCH AS THE DOOR flew open and two young boys sprang out, closely followed by a wiry man of medium height.

Flashing her a smile, Harry rubbed a work-roughened hand over his balding head. "Welcome home, love. Got a bit damp, hey?"

She handed him the baby basket with its slumbering, precious cargo and wrinkled her nose. "Just a little. Have the boys been good?"

"Of course. They gave me a hand to get the cows in and feed the calves." He gazed fondly at the two grubby faces. "You're my special helpers, aren't you?"

George and Timmy nodded, and Alice's heart swelled with love for her sons. At seven and five respectively, they believed they were indispensable to their father—perfectly capable of doing a man's job—and neither she nor Harry would ever disappoint them by indicating otherwise.

"Come on then. We'd better stoke the fire and get you into the bath." She met her husband's doting glance. "Is Paddy still at the shed?"

Harry nodded. "He's washing down the yard and will be in directly. I'll leave you to it then and see to the horse."

"Thanks, love. He's eating the hay left in the feeder." Her husband tugged an oilskin coat over his shirt and trousers and pulled a weather-beaten felt hat over his ears.

The rain was steady now, but in the distance a faded rainbow hovered over the estuary. The days were lengthening, thankfully. More daylight meant Harry and his cowman, Paddy, could remain outside and complete the additional chores winter had seen them put on hold. With the impending move to the new farm, there were many preparations to be made.

Alice breathed a sigh of relief, secretly grateful the men would be late coming inside. It meant she could prepare the evening meal and feed the children without tripping over two pairs of legs extending from beneath the kitchen table.

After closing the door tightly behind her, she grabbed a block of firewood and used it to stoke the fireplace embers. When the children's playful shrieks sounded from the hallway and the baby woke with a wail, she scooped him up and onto her hip and waved a scolding finger at his brothers. "Settle down now. Go and fetch a piece of wood each while I get the water ready."

The boys shared a grin and raced outside to the porch where the wood box sat out of the weather against the side wall. By the time they returned, their mother, still jiggling the bellowing baby, had the water dribbling into the old enamel bathtub.

Her divided attention flicked from John to the taps

protruding through the wall, relieved to see only water flowing into the tub. No frogs or lumps of rust appeared as had happened before—to her dismay, and in the case of frogs, to the delight of her sons. One pipe trickled cold water directly from the tank outside, while the other spluttered and coughed, finally divesting itself of a half-hearted stream from the wet-back: a small tank attached to the rear of the kitchen fire.

Without hesitation, George and Timmy stripped off and climbed into the tub. At the gasps and squeals on sinking into the tepid water, Alice's guilt surged. The fire had been ignored for over two hours, so the water would not yet have reached a comfortable warmth. Bath time would be quick.

"Hurry now and wash yourselves before you get cold." She handed George a well-used bar of soap and a small towelling washcloth, then sat on the stool next to the bath and put John to her breast. As his wailing turned to snuffles and then silence, she stroked her baby's fine blond hair and gazed into his bright blue eyes.

He was so like Emmie.

If their daughter had survived, what she would look like now?

Swallowing the lump in her throat, Alice continued gazing at her youngest, who gurgled happily back at her, milk dribbling from the side of his mouth.

While the boys splashed and played in the tub, she pondered the decision she and Harry had made to move to a bigger farm. It was the right choice, one that would offer their family better opportunities. And it had always been Harry's dream to be a sheep and beef-cattle farmer.

For over ten years, they had slogged to repay the debt on this dairy farm—the farm that Harry's father had purchased while his son was in Egypt, fighting for his country. Now his parents had passed on, and the worry about offending his father was irrelevant.

Alice had thought her greatest stumbling block to relocating was being forced to leave Emmie behind, but regardless of her father's words, she now realised that it had never been about Emmie. What had kept her bound to their old life was a sense of duty to both sets of parents—an obligation to follow instructions, dutifully visit, share food, and labour, and accept that they knew best.

An obligation that was now, no longer a consideration.

CHAPTER 2

As pale fingers of dawn crept into a watery sky, Harry took the wooden box from Alice's hands and shoved it into place on the floor of the old truck.

"I hope it will be enough?" she said.

"It will. You're a great cook, Alice Simpson. Why else do you think I married you?" He grinned and lifted the damp tea towel, nodding appreciatively. "Good to see you didn't forget the most important item."

She burst into laughter. "I wouldn't dare."

The box was filled with jars containing mutton stew, a pat of butter, bread, six apples, and Harry's favourite—rice pudding. Two enamel plates, mugs, and cutlery were neatly wrapped in a tea towel and tucked next to the tin billy cans.

Harry hoisted George onto the passenger seat then leaned over and hugged her, planting a gentle kiss on her lips. "We'll see you in three days." He opened the driver's door and climbed in.

Alice's heart lurched as the engine coughed, whined, and kicked into life.

The pony tethered to the frame behind the cab pawed at the floor beneath his hooves. Surrounded by fence posts, wire, chicken netting, drums of diesel, and a wooden dog kennel, the little black gelding flicked his tail and stamped impatiently.

A dog perched on the roof of the kennel, its golden coat glistening in the early sunlight. His back was flecked with a dark patch resembling a saddle, and floppy ears hung like a setter's from either side of his head. Neither a Collie nor a Huntaway, his heritage was questionable. To Harry he was simply a good, faithful dog and he'd named him Rock. The dog's lips quivered as though attempting a smile, and his tail wagged with anticipation.

"Bye, Mum," George called as he leaned out the open window while the truck rolled forward. "And stop making that din, Stormy!" he admonished the pony.

Alice smiled softly and waved, swallowing her anxiety as the vehicle lumbered down the driveway and turned onto the road. She stood until long after the noise of the diesel engine faded, until her reverie was broken by the bellowing of cows squelching up the lane to the milking shed. A wizened little man hobbled along the track behind them, his bow-legged gait a legacy of childhood malnourishment and a hard life. He lifted an arm to Alice, and she waved back as a door banged.

"When are we going to Aunty Maudie's?" Timmy stood on the porch in his pyjamas, his face alight with anticipation.

"After breakfast." She walked to him and rested her hand on her son's shoulder. "Let's get you dressed now."

Within minutes, the boy was sitting at the kitchen table, shovelling porridge into his mouth as though it was his last meal. Alice propped John in the wooden highchair and stirred the gruel while the baby bashed a spoon on the tray. Chortling, he leaned forward, opening his mouth like a hungry bird as she ladled the food onto the pink tongue. She glanced at Timmy. "Slow down. You might choke."

He looked at her for a second before lifting the bowl to his mouth and drinking the remaining milky mixture. Shaking her head, she stifled a grin. Instilling good table manners into young boys was a challenge no one had mentioned before she had her own, but she secretly appreciated the spirit that Timmy showed. George was different—quiet, serious, and measured in both his actions and thoughts. It was too early to know what John's temperament would be. So far, Alice could only hope that his smiling, placid nature and interest in the animals continued.

———

AN HOUR LATER, HARNESSED TO THE BUGGY, DUKE waited patiently in the yard while Alice placed a small leather suitcase in the storage box behind the seat. "Where's your hat?"

The boy was pressing the end of a stick into the patches of mud created by last night's rain, and she frowned.

He looked blankly at her and shrugged. "Dunno."

"It'll be on the wood box, most likely. Quick. Run and fetch it or we'll be late."

While he sprinted back to the porch, Alice settled John in the baby basket, stuffed a cushion behind his back, and offered him a crust of bread to gnaw on. She tucked the food basket into a corner on the floor and untied the reins.

Duke stood motionless, facing the house as though he knew why he must wait, then flicked his head as Timmy ran towards them, hat in hand and an expression of surprised jubilation on his face. "Got it!"

Reaching down, Alice grasped him by the arm and hauled him into the buggy. "Good boy. Everybody ready?" She looked at her sons and smiled.

"Let's go." Timmy bounced and shot a cheeky grin at his mother.

Alice flicked the reins. "Walk up, Duke."

The morning sun glistened on the grass along the

roadside as the horse settled into a rhythmic trot, quickly eating up the miles.

Just before half past nine, he dropped back to a walk, turned down a narrow lane, and followed the hydrangea-lined driveway to a white, low-set house.

"They're here!" Shrieks greeted them as they drew to a halt near the front path. Two boys and a girl streaked across the lawn and jumped up and down next to the buggy.

"Settle down, you lot!" The command came from a woman of such similar build and appearance to Alice, it was obvious they had to be sisters—or even twins: small, blond-haired, and with a nose that, like Alice's, was just a little too big to be considered pretty. She wore a floral dress partially covered with an apron, and as she approached the gathering, she held out her arms. "Pass the little fellow to me."

Alice handed the baby over, while Timmy leaped off the buggy and joined the others in a race towards the house.

"You'd never guess they see each other every week," Alice said, smiling. She gave her sister a hug and Maud, perching the baby on her hip, reached up to take the basket of food.

"What have you got in this, Alice? It weighs a ton."

Alice grinned and ignored her sister's question. "Thanks for having Timmy for me, Maudie. Without him, I'll have packed up the house and will be ready and waiting when Harry and George get home on

Tuesday evening." Alice felt a tug on her skirt and her eyes dropped to the little girl standing next to her. She bent and picked her up, allowing the thin arms to creep around her neck as blonde curls brushed against Alice's cheek.

"How is my special little girl?" she whispered. Catherine was the odd one out, and as though trying to make up for Emmie's absence, her adoration for her aunt and young cousin, John, were as obvious as the moon on a clear night.

"Good," Catherine whispered back.

Alice cleared her throat and pinned a smile on her face.

It didn't seem to matter how often she held Maud's daughter, she could never shake the ache deep inside her—the wish that this child was her own Emmie. The girls had been born only three weeks apart, and yet miraculously, all of Maud's children had evaded the dreaded whooping cough that had swept through the community while her own little Emmie had succumbed to the disease at three months of age. Now she was at peace, and Alice was grateful for the survival of her two older sons and the unexpected arrival of John. She knew what her father did not. There would be no more.

She set the child down and passed her a small paper bag. "Do you think you can carry that for me? It's got a special surprise in it for you to share." She lowered her voice to a whisper. "Barley sugars."

Maud met Alice's eyes, her eyebrows raised. The boiled sweets were a treat for all, purchased on special occasions—and Alice considered leaving the only district she had ever known one of those.

Turning to the buggy again, Alice ignored her sister's frown and unloaded the suitcase. "I won't stay long, Maud. Just a cup of tea and a piece of your delicious sponge cake and John and I will be off again …

"Hello there!" A broad Scottish accent boomed across the lawn and a stocky man with a shock of red hair strode towards them. "I'll see to the horse and be in shortly." He gave Alice a peck on the cheek before turning to Maud and kissing her. "Better not let my wife get jealous." His laugh rumbled from deep within as he took the horse's reins and led him away.

"Thanks, Dougal," Alice called after him, shaking her head and smiling. Her brother-in-law's affection for his wife and children was as clear as daylight—and his love of horses followed close behind. It was his accent that continued to throw her. In spite of having left his homeland as a teenager, his conversations were, for her, as hard to understand as when they'd first met a decade ago.

———

THE SISTERS SAT ACROSS THE TABLE FROM ONE ANOTHER, dregs of tea lining the bottom of the delicate bone china cups and a plate of crumbs all that remained of a delicious, cream-filled sponge cake. The boys had long since been despatched outside to play and Dougal returned to the fields. Catherine sat on the floor with John, making towers with wooden blocks then allowing the baby to knock them down again, setting them both off in a fit of giggles.

"I know you're upset with me." Maud clasped her empty cup with both hands as she looked up and shrugged. "I didn't think you'd really do it … I thought we'd live the rest of our lives as we do now, with only a few miles separating us. But it's only days away, and I'm really sorry I haven't shown you much support." Maud's voice cracked, and Alice reached across the table and took her hand.

"I understand. I can't quite believe it either, but Harry assures me the journey can be made in a day and as the roads improve, we can be together for special occasions." She squeezed Maud's fingers.

"So, is there much more for you to do?"

Alice frowned as her mind raced. "Not really. Except for the kitchen and pantry, we don't have a lot. The linen chest is already packed, and I've put lavender and mothballs amongst the blankets—so it's only our personal possessions and clothes." She hesitated, unable to disguise the anxiety in her tone. "I wish I could help with getting the sheep to the farm though."

Maud's frown mimicked Alice's own. "What do you mean?"

"Well, Harry will have to go ahead of the mob to

prepare things at the other end. You know, make sure gates are open and there's no broken fences or anything."

"So … what makes you think you need to be there?"

"George. He'll ride behind the sheep from Helensville with only the dog for assistance. Harry will drive back to help him once things are ready at the farm. It's just … I don't know. He's only seven, and to me he's still a little boy."

"I know what you mean." Maud patted Alice's hand and continued reassuringly, "He's a competent rider though, and Harry would not put him in any danger. Anyway, it's not as though he has much choice really, does he?"

"I suppose not. And Rock is a good dog." Her voice wavered as she attempted to justify her comments. "He'll control the flock and look out for his young master." She smiled at Maud and attempted to change the subject. "George is very excited about the little saddle Dougal gave him. He thinks he's as good as one of the men now."

Maud smiled softly. "In Dougal's opinion, he needs one for safety. So he can get on and off his pony more easily if he has to." She paused, narrowing her eyes. "Why didn't Harry take the sheep you already own?"

Alice met Maud's gaze—one filled with more of a lack of understanding than reproach.

The decisions she and Harry had made continued to create questions and criticism within her extended family. At times, she had struggled to resist the urge to give them all a tongue lashing and instead had forced an understanding smile.

"The new buyer offered a fair price for the farm as a going concern. So they get the dairy cows, our little flock, the two horses, and most of the furniture as well as the property. I thought I'd told you all that?" She straightened in her chair.

"You did. I'm sorry I asked. It's none of my business, and I suppose I didn't listen to you properly the first time."

Alice gave her a gentle smile. "It was a good opportunity to buy young Romney sheep anyway, so the agent arranged for five hundred to be transported from down Te Kuiti way to Helensville. They're being sent by train then yarded until Harry collects them … and because there's not much of an alternative, it makes more sense to walk them the twenty miles." She hesitated for a moment. "Apparently, there's a telephone line that goes to most of the farms, so maybe we'll be able to phone each other occasionally?"

Maud snorted. "Of course we can—one day. Toll calls are out of our budget though, and I can't imagine yours will be any better in this decade, or the next."

Alice chuckled at her sister's pessimistic remark and reached instead for her basket, withdrawing the gift she had brought. She passed the parcel wrapped in brown paper across the table and chewed the inside of her cheek while surprise flooded Maud's round face.

"What's this?"

"Just a little something for you to help close the gap between us." Alice shot her a small smile. "Open it."

Maud carefully untied the piece of ribbon from the package and removed the paper. She raised her eyebrows and fingered the contents before her face softened and she met Alice's eyes. "Writing paper, envelopes, and a new fountain pen. I think this is telling me something?" She chuckled, slowly allowing it to grow to a full-bellied laugh that bordered on hysteria.

Alice joined in as they simultaneously stood and moved around the table to hug each other. The bond between the sisters, barely a year apart in age, was strong. It would take more than a day's journey and a domineering family to drive them apart.

"I bought one for each of us when we went to Papakura last week. We will write regularly, even if there's no mail collection. I don't mind if I get a pile of letters all at once."

Maud nodded. "I'll begin my first letter while Dougal is driving Timmy back to you on Tuesday."

"It's a promise. And I'll write to you the minute we arrive." The women looked at each other. "Well, as soon as I have time anyway," Alice added. She glanced at the clock on the mantlepiece. "I'd better be off. Come on, little man." She reached and joisted John onto her hip, and then kissed Catherine's cheek.

Minutes later, having given stern instructions to

Timmy to behave himself, Alice climbed into the buggy. She looked at Maud and bit her quivering lip.

"Don't you dare," Maud ordered. "If you start, you'll have me blubbering too."

Alice gave her a watery smile and nodded as she urged Duke into a walk.

"Don't forget—write every single week," Maud called after her.

Alice waved and yelled as the tears ran down her face, "I won't!"

———

"Where would you like me to put the boxes, Mrs Alice?"

She banged her head on the shelf at Paddy's unexpected question and withdrew from the pantry's recesses. Wrapping and packing the precious jars of preserved fruit, jams, and pickles had been a bigger job than she had expected, and having filled two wooden crates with the products, she discovered they were too heavy to lift. Alice rubbed her temples, wrinkling her brow before answering. "Thank you, Paddy. Um, perhaps you could stack them on the porch next to the wood box if there's enough room?"

The little Irishman touched his forehead and gave a nod before picking up a crate, barely pausing. Brushing the dust off her apron, Alice stretched her back and watched him go. *You're an unusual fellow.*

She followed him to the porch as he shifted the final box. "Thank you." With the exception of the bare necessities, their belongings were packed and stored either in the sitting room or along the walls of the back porch, ready for loading onto the truck.

"I hope the new fella is as good to me as you and Harry, Mrs Alice."

Alice studied the sad, wrinkled face and, unexpectedly, a lump formed in her throat. It had taken years to convince Paddy to drop the 'Mr' prefix from Harry's name, but somehow he seemed unable to do the same for her.

She took a slow breath and gave him a reassuring smile. "I'm sure he will be, but you only have to stay for two weeks to help him settle in and then you're free to go to any of the Simpson farms. You will always have a home with one of us, and you might even consider coming up to South Head in time? From what Harry says, there'll be no shortage of work there."

Alice waited while the little man fidgeted with the hat in his hands. "Right then. I'll go and fetch the cows. Harry and George will be back shortly." He turned and was gone.

She closed the door and gazed out the window as he hobbled away. A wave of concern gnawed at her insides.

Paddy had turned up looking for work soon after they married, and in spite of helping on both Harry's and his siblings' farms, years had slipped by with no one knowing his background. As far as Harry was concerned, it didn't matter. He preferred to take people as he found them, and as long as they were willing to learn, everyone was happy. When Alice was struggling to manage Duke, Paddy had been her guiding hand until she made the mistake of asking him where he had gained his knowledge. His response had both intrigued and confused her. *"If you ask no questions, you'll be told no lies."* After that, he barely spoke for days.

She sighed and returned to the kitchen, anxious to achieve as much as possible while John slept.

———

Darkness was falling quickly, and Alice had just finished feeding John when a rumble signalled the approach of a heavy vehicle. She froze, listening intently, praying it didn't pass by. No, the engine slowed, followed by a second vehicle changing down gears, and her heart skipped a beat. She plucked the baby from his highchair and hurried outside, her smile spreading as Harry and George waved enthusiastically out of the windows of the approaching truck. Following close behind was a bright red Bedford, its timber crate on the back looming over the vehicle's glossy cab. Behind the wheel, Dougal's auburn hair shone like a beacon, and beside him, Timmy's tiny shadow sprang to life as the vehicles ground to a halt.

CHAPTER 3

South Head
Helensville
7 November 1935

My dearest Maud,

We have arrived. It was an uneventful journey and the children coped well, probably better than me as the road was very hilly and with so many twists and turns, I felt sick. We stopped in Helensville and explored the town while Harry saw to business matters, and my first impressions are good. It's a pretty area, quite steep with many nice kauri cottages and villas built along the hillside overlooking the harbour. Harry said this was quite a large logging area, supplying kauri timber to Auckland by boat. The town has a grocer, drapery, post office, bank, and all the necessary stockists of farm supplies. The main employer appears to be the Kaipara Dairy Company, and on our way to South Head, about five miles from Helensville, we passed a few buildings they call Parakai Springs, which houses a thermal bathhouse and seems to be attracting a number of visitors.

I know you'll be dying to hear about our new home—and I can imagine your questions, so I'll do my best. The land is steeper and rougher than what we are used to, but the views are beautiful. From the top of the hill, near where we will build our house, we can see the Tasman ocean to the west and overlook the Kaipara Harbour on the east. There are two boats that traverse the Kaipara from Helensville to Dargaville on a regular basis and provide both a passenger and cargo service, although apparently not for flocks of sheep. In spite of the tea tree that seems to grow anywhere and everywhere, the rolling and flatter areas of the farm are relatively clear, and I can now see why it appealed to Harry. There are also a number of flowing springs providing good water, which is a bonus.

Our 'house' is a corrugated iron shed. It's solid but primitive and has no evidence of a woman's touch, so I suppose that's now my job! Behind the main shed (which appears to be a forge and workshop), there is a room big enough to divide in half, allowing Harry and I to use the smaller portion as our bedroom and the rest to be our kitchen and living area. A small hearth and open fire are the only cooking facilities, but we're investigating the purchase of a wood stove with an oven as making bread is difficult without one. I have to put the loaf in a cast-iron pot with hot coals on the lid, just like our old cook used to do when we were small.

Anyway, back to our living quarters. On the side of the

shed there's a second room added on which the previous owner used as a bedroom. It's big enough for the boys and when our house has been built, can be used as accommodation for shearers or other workers. The wash house is next to it with a copper, tubs, and enough room to house a bath. I'm glad Harry had thought to purchase an enamel bathtub before we arrived. I didn't like to ask how the previous residents kept themselves clean—a bucket maybe? A few yards from the shed, there's a water tank with a storeroom on its southern side and an outhouse toilet at the end. The storeroom is quite cool inside as it has some wire gauze panelling. Perfect for preserves, fruit, and vegetables—and of course meat and milk. Harry has made enquiries about buying a house cow from a nearby farmer and meanwhile will build a milking bale and fence off a small paddock for her. Until then, we will continue using powdered milk.

The last ten miles of our journey was along a narrow but quite well-formed road, and I should be able to manage Duke and the buggy on it when they eventually arrive. Our furniture was sent by boat from Helensville and delivered to the little wharf on the Kaipara Harbour side of our farm. I haven't seen it yet, but Harry said a man called Ed lives in a shack by the wharf and seems to manage the comings and goings. He allows locals to leave mail, which is collected by boat or barge when they come, so I guess he is our mailman? It seems a sensible solution. Ed and one of the young bachelors (there are two who live within a few miles of our farm— Clive Thuragood and Vince Williamson), helped Harry get the piano off the barge and onto the truck—and then unloaded it at this end. A tricky business, and I had visions of it being smashed to pieces. However, it is safe and remains in tune—sort of, anyway.

We have walked over much of the farm as the weather has been lovely. Behind the shed/living quarters and covering the hillside to the south is a large area of native bush. The boys and I found a track through it and were amazed at the birds—a lot of friendly fantails and we even saw a kereru. The farm doesn't have a name, so I am thinking of calling it Fantail Ridge. Don't you think it's a pretty name?

I miss you all and our weekly get-togethers. It will be about two years before we can begin the house, so until then, I hope we can return occasionally to see you. The telephone is a wonderful thing. However, there are about ten farms connected to the one shared line, so privacy would be doubtful—and the line itself is a piece of wire stretched for miles across the mud flats and is often out of order after strong winds or heavy rain. I'll be restricting my use of it to essential communication and for ordering stores, so knowing we can receive and send mail from here is a great relief. No power or running water, I can cope with but would feel isolated without some sort of contact.

There is so much I want to tell you, but I need to prepare our evening meal.

I look forward to receiving your letter.

Much love to you all,

Alice

Alice licked the stamp and carefully addressed the

envelope, then wrote a grocery order in her clear, flowing handwriting. Picking up both letter and list, she placed them on the kitchen dresser before continuing into the bedroom to check on her sleeping baby. She paused beside the beautiful carvings on the headboard of their bed, and reaching out, ran her hand over the rich, rimu timber. Robert, Harry's elder brother, had made the bed for them as a wedding present, spending many long evenings working in his shed, according to his wife. Alice reflected on the day the bed was gifted to them. Her father had raised his bushy eyebrows, and his grim face sent a queasy feeling through her. In her strict, Protestant upbringing, beds were for sleeping in and no adornment was necessary —but she loved the intricate leaves and swirls that wound their way up the slats on both ends of the beautiful piece of furniture.

―――――

"I'm heading down to see Ed about ordering a mullet net." Harry stood in the wash house doorway.

Balancing the sheet on a wooden stick as it was swallowed by the mangle, Alice dared not turn her head, her concentration glued to the water flowing back into the boiling-hot copper.

"Is there anything you need?" Harry spoke again quietly.

The sheet dropped into the rinse water and she

turned and beamed at him. His patience was, for her, one of his most attractive attributes—perhaps second only to his insistence that they were equal. Even the solicitor had blinked repeatedly when Harry insisted the new property be registered in both their names.

"Yes please. Can you take my letters? I'll get them for you." She hesitated. "Did you say mullet net?"

He nodded.

"Apparently, the harbour is loaded with them—mullet, I mean. Vince said he's got a net and has built a smoke house so he can eat the fish fresh or smoked. Even if we only get a few from time to time, they will give us variety and save me having to kill a sheep as often."

"Sounds good to me."

———

TO ALICE'S DELIGHT, BARELY A WEEK LATER, A LIGHT green Chevrolet truck grumbled up the hill from the direction of the wharf, revs and gear changes heralding its arrival outside the gate. A horn sounded three times, and Alice hurried across the soon-to-be house paddock.

"Mrs Simpson?" A wide grin lit up the fresh, young face. Pushing his hat towards the back of his head, the man scratched the thatch of curly brown hair. He wasn't particularly tall, but nevertheless, she had to tip her head back to meet his eyes.

"That's me." Alice returned his smile as excitement warmed her.

"I'm Clive—from the farm next door to Vince." He pulled a packet of tobacco from his pocket and began rolling a cigarette.

"Oh. Nice to meet you."

Alice waited while he lit his rollup, pushed it to the side of his mouth, and clamped his lips over it. Then he threw the canvas tarpaulin back that covered the rear tray, revealing a load of assorted boxes and parcels.

"I brought your mail and groceries. Had to collect mine, so thought it would be a good opportunity to say hello."

He passed her a brown paper bundle tied with string and she clutched it to her chest, her insides fluttering with anticipation. While she rubbed one leg against the back of the other, he re-covered the truck's contents then leaned against the passenger door.

After removing the cigarette from his mouth, he flicked the drooping grey ash onto the road and glanced upwards.

"We'll have rain before the day's out."

Alice blinked into the cloudless sky. "Really? W-would you like a cup of tea?"

"No thank you, Mrs Simpson. I'll carry these groceries inside for you and then be getting along." He threw his cigarette down and ground it out under his boot before picking up a crate filled with tins of milk powder, a box of tea, flour, sugar, and a few canned goods.

They walked to the kitchen in comfortable silence, and Alice ushered him inside. He placed the box on the scrubbed wooden table, tipped his hat at her, and retreated the way he had come. "See you again."

"Yes, thank you. You and Vince must come and have tea with us some time," she said.

"We'd love to."

"Next Sunday?"

"Perfect. Shall I speak to Vince? I'm calling to drop his mail off as well."

She twisted her lips momentarily. It wasn't proper for an invitation to come via a third party. But on the other hand, communication wasn't always simple in the country. "That would be wonderful. I look forward to seeing you both on Sunday evening."

He raised his hand in acknowledgement, and she waved back. As the truck drove away, she grabbed the bundle of mail from the table and whipped off the string. Two newspapers, an official-looking letter addressed to Harry, and a small white envelope addressed in Maud's writing. She ripped it open and eagerly began to read.

Innisfree
Kingseat
29 October 1935

My dearest Alice,

I am sitting at the table where only days ago we shared tea and cake together and can't believe that you have really gone.

As Dougal will have told you, Timmy was no trouble while staying here, and the boys thoroughly enjoyed spending time together. They helped plant potatoes and pick peas, and I hope the bag full of vegetables he's delivering will keep you going until you can get your garden established. Some of the spuds have already shot, so you need to get them in now. The box of cloth bags contains bulbs and seeds. I hope they grow on your new farm and you get enough rain?

Catherine has been moping around as though she has lost her only friend, so I suggested she draw a picture for you— enclosed here. Apparently, it is a picture of you and John with Duke.

Speaking of Duke, I also hope he arrives safely together with your buggy. Dougal will take them into Papakura sometime in the next fortnight to be despatched as arranged with Harry.

We missed you at Church on Sunday. Mrs Webster offered to play the piano, but she is not a patch on you. At times it was hard to even recognise the hymn she was play-ing, but fortunately we were able to drown her out with our singing. During morning tea afterwards, there was discus-sion over how we will cope without such a talented pianist, but no doubt someone will come forth. I would offer, but I don't play as well as you and balk at the thought of being

*criticised. I hope your piano arrived in one piece and you
have a safe and dry place to store it?*

*I can't think of anything else to tell you and am looking
forward to receiving your letter and hearing all about your
new home. I miss you!*

Sending my love to you all,

Your loving sister,

Maud

Alice looked up and blinked. Through misty eyes,
she glanced around the makeshift room, her gaze
resting on the piano. It sat on smooth kauri planks
against the wooden partition that divided the
machinery side of the shed from their quarters. She
had used her father's wedding gift of a hundred pounds
to purchase the black Steinway, and her face softened
at the memory. Her older sisters had suggested she buy
something useful and practical—something like a
dining table and chairs. However, Harry was insistent
that she spend the money on whatever might give her a
lifetime of pleasure. She had done exactly that.

She lay the letter on the table and moved to the
tapestry-covered stool, then, lifting the heavy lid, ran
her fingers up and down the keyboard, limbering her
knuckles as the tone seeped into her soul. Chuckling at
Maud's reference to being criticised, she shook her
head. Wasn't that exactly what Maud was doing to Mrs
Webster? She flexed her fingers and began playing
'Sweet Bye and Bye', the song that when her mother

was alive, and Alice had sat beside her in the old sitting room, had been her favourite.

"Mum!" The high-pitched child's voice reclaimed her attention with a jolt, and she glanced up. Timmy stood in the doorway, his face and hands covered with dirt.

"Oh dear. Where have you been?"

"Helping Dad." Timmy tilted his head to one side as though puzzled that his mother would even ask. "We've been digging postholes."

Alice grimaced as a wail sounded from the behind the curtain, indicating the end of John's nap. Imagining how helpful Timmy had been, she picked up the baby and reached for a cloth. A bucket stood by the door, filled with water for hand washing as the workers, large and small, entered the house. Alice had been about to refresh it when Clive arrived, and now she peered into the cloudy, brown liquid. She shrugged, dampened the cloth, and wiped it over Timmy's face. He squirmed, protesting loudly.

"What is it with you boys? You know the rules. Everyone washes when they come in from work."

The little boy rolled his eyes and plunged his hands into the bucket. "Do you want to see what we've been doing?"

"I would love to." She slipped off her shoes and stepped into gumboots, John's legs gripping tightly around her waist as she lifted each foot. In spite of the dry weather, the ability to slip the knee-high rubber boots on and off easily made them her preferred outdoor footwear—and the added bonus was the long grass couldn't tickle her bare legs.

She followed Timmy outside, pausing as she gazed down the paddock and heaved a sigh. There was so much to do here.

Harry was adamant the peninsula was full of promises and, in time, was certain Fantail Ridge would be considerably more lucrative than their dairy farm in the rich, fertile fields of Karaka. But Alice had reservations. *Perhaps it's because my family focus on negatives, or perhaps it's because I doubt my own capabilities.* Either way, she accepted the control her father and siblings exuded, with little if any praise offered, had clouded her confidence. Life with Harry was different. He was positive, enthusiastic, and he appreciated everything she did.

Timmy pushed open the picket gate and ran towards his father and brother, and she strode purposefully behind him.

Don't dwell on the past. This is our chance, and we're a team.

CHAPTER 4

The field was barely five acres and sloped away from the ridge, with native bush lining the long side and a row of small macrocarpa trees across the western edge facing the Tasman. Harry had planted them during one of his visits prior to the move, claiming they would provide good protection from the winds that howled over the peninsula—and of course shelter their home and sheds. In time, Alice thought they might plant pine trees on the road boundary and perhaps a nice pittosporum hedge to border the garden.

Lifting his head from his front paws, Rock thumped his tail on the ground as Alice and Timmy approached.

"How is the fencing going?" Alice stifled a grin as she met Harry's gaze.

His blue eyes sparkled, like sapphires in rich brown earth, while his handsome face wore a trail of mud down one cheek. "Nearly done, thanks to my trusty helpers." He ruffled George's hair. "The posts are in, and we've done the wire on this side. Now we'll get the battens on and should have the paddock secure by tomorrow evening."

"Then the cow can come?" she asked hopefully. Powdered milk was pleasant enough, but she was itching to have fresh milk and cream for butter making. It was a tasty alternative to the dripping they spread on bread each day, and she looked forward to making scones and pancakes with the buttermilk.

"Hopefully. She's due to calve, so won't be long now."

"Clive just delivered the grocery order and mail," Alice announced.

Harry put down the hammer and leaned on a post. "And …?"

"Newspapers and letters, including one from Maud." Her face lit up.

"Well then, I won't need to take you to town after all?" Harry chuckled as disappointment clouded Alice's face. He stepped forward and gave her a hug. "You know I wouldn't do that. We'll try to get into Helensville every few weeks and hope that a neighbour or the boats can bring the mail and anything else we need in between times."

Alice gave him a gentle shove. "You'd better. Remember your promise?"

He grinned again and said softly, "Of course I do."

"Oh, I nearly forgot. I've invited Clive and Vince for tea on Sunday night."

Before Harry could answer, Rock barked, and Alice glanced anxiously at the sky, following his gaze. Her eyes narrowed as she focused on the large bird circling high above them. There were not many predators in New Zealand, and once her hens grew to full size, they would be safe, but as half-grown pullets they were still in danger. A hungry hawk would not hesitate to swoop down and carry one off to make a tasty meal for its family. She hitched John more firmly on her hip and strolled over to the mesh pens under the pohutukawa tree. She had brought with them a rooster and four hens, plus eight chickens from the most recent hatching. They were several weeks old now, and she kept her fingers crossed that soon they would be adding to the family's egg supply.

Lowering John onto a patch of shorter, soft grass, she reached up to remove the washing flapping above her head. The clothesline was nothing more than a sagging piece of wire that ran from a post in the middle of the paddock across to a tree at the edge of the bush. Alice had to run a cloth over it every time she wanted to use it, wiping away the bird droppings and traces of rust that would ruin their clothes. After throwing the towels over her shoulder, she picked John up again and made her way back to the shed.

———

It was the last week in November, and Alice gazed across the paddock at their accomplishments. The fence was complete, chickens were scratching around in the new fowl run, the rusty clothesline had been replaced by a clean run of new wire, and the cow bale stood proudly in the corner, waiting for an occupant.

In Alice's opinion, the most exciting event since their arrival had been the delivery of the wood stove. Surprisingly, Harry had sourced it second hand during a recent trip to town. It wasn't perfect, but it had an oven and a good-sized fire box, which meant Alice could again produce cakes and casseroles—and of course rice puddings. She'd scrubbed the patches of rust from it and given it a generous coating of stove black. Now it had been used and cleaned a few times, it functioned as well as a brand-new one might.

Warm, dry weather had settled over the peninsula and, while Harry continued to divide the huge paddocks with never-ending posts and rolls of wire, Alice dug and planted Maud's potatoes, grinning as she pushed them into the ground and imagining her sister's instructions, had she been here. As children, they had planted potatoes together and, while Maud lined each of hers in perfectly straight rows exactly the same distance apart, Alice made patterns with her quota, zigzagging them along the mounded earth as she went, delighting in successfully annoying her sister.

"Alice!" An unusually anxious note in Harry's voice snapped Alice out of her reverie and she rushed around the corner of the shed, drying her hands on her apron and almost crashing into her husband.

"Oh, there you are." He paused for a moment, panting, and Alice glanced across the grass to the horse tied to their front gate, its rider strolling towards them.

"What's the matter?"

Harry inclined his head towards the approaching stranger.

"Apparently, the phone is out. This young man has brought a message for us to collect the horse and buggy from Helensville."

"That's great ... isn't it?"

The rider drew close. Alice smiled warmly, noting the gangly young man's hesitation as he removed his hat and fidgeted.

"My wife, Alice," Harry said. "And this is Reg Ainsworth—from the big house a few miles back."

"Would you like to come in for a cup of tea?" Alice was delighted to see a new face in spite of Harry's puzzled expression.

"Thank you, but no. I'd better be getting home. We've just finished shearing, and there's a bit to do," Reg said.

"A glass of water then?"

"Thank you. That would be very kind."

Alice turned and hurried inside, filled a glass with cool water, and cut a slice of the freshly baked madeira cake.

As she handed the plate and glass to the young man,

he shot her a wide grin. "Thank you, Mrs Simpson. There's not too many messages we pass on that get this response."

"You're very welcome." She chuckled.

"We'll get into town tomorrow and collect the horse and buggy. Thank you very much for coming all this way to let us know," Harry said.

Confusion shadowed Reg's face as he swallowed a mouthful of cake.

"I was told it was horses. Plural. I didn't ask how many."

Alice and Harry looked at each other before Harry replied. "There must be a mistake. We only have one horse. Duke. Sadly we had to leave ours on the property we sold as they were part of the deal."

Reg shrugged. "Sorry, that's all I know."

"Oh well, we'll sort it out tomorrow." Harry reached to shake the young man's hand. "Thanks again for coming all this way."

He mounted and swung the horse away, kicking it into a trot as he descended the steep track.

Alice met Harry's eyes.

"I guess we get organised for a trip to town in the morning then. It seems that's the only way we'll know."

Her heart skipped a beat, certain that an outing would be the highlight of her week.

Fantail Ridge
South Head
3 December 1935

MY DEAREST MAUD,

I am hurrying this letter in order to catch the barge today and have so much to tell you. The enclosed note is from Harry to Dougal, expressing our thanks for his help.

The son of a neighbour (living a few miles closer to Helensville than ourselves) rode over to advise us of the arrival of Duke and our buggy in town, so yesterday we were up before daybreak, got our chores done, and piled in the truck. I know it's only twenty miles, but the road is nothing like what you and I are used to. It's really a winding track over hills, with tight corners and a few flat stretches in between—just enough for us to recover a little before our stomachs get left behind on the next hill. I imagine those flat areas will be boggy in winter as the tide comes over them in several places!

We went to the stock yards, where Duke gave me a wonderful welcome and I was delighted to see that the label around his neck had my name on it, not Harry's. Thanks, Dougal! However, Duke was not alone as a very nice bay gelding was in the same yard and Harry's name was on his tag! We have no idea where or from whom he came—only that he was delivered to the Papakura yards for transport to Harry shortly after Dougal left Duke and the buggy there— so they must have put two and two together and decided he was meant for us? Very odd indeed, and I guess now we'll have to write to the manager at Papakura and see what we can find out. The horse has a broad white stripe down his face, so needless to say, we have called him Blaze. Harry believes him to be around five or six years old judging by his teeth, and although not shod, he has strong legs and sound hooves.

While in town, we enjoyed a stroll up the main street, and I visited both the grocer and the drapery. The early fruit is coming in now, and we bought a box of plums. Guess what I will be doing for the next few days? I also purchased a piece of floral material to make myself a new dress and a few yards of blue cotton for clothes for the boys. My sewing machine is still wrapped up in the corner of the shed, but Harry said he will move it into our bedroom for me so I can sew. We had lunch in the tea rooms, which was very exciting for us all (egg sandwiches and little fairy cakes—delicious but not as good as yours). The tea room is called 'Why Not'— a wonderfully fitting name, don't you think? The boys had lemon cordial, and of course Harry and I never say no to a pot of tea.

Our trip home was not without its issues. After harnessing Duke, we tied Blaze to the back of the buggy and I tried to set off, but the silly horse refused to move! Harry was concerned he would break the halter and hurt himself, so we ended up having to put him on the truck. Not quite what we expected, especially as the sides are low and if he pulled away, he could easily have jumped off. However, he stood still and seemed to enjoy his sightseeing tour of South Head all the way home. No doubt we provided some much-appre-

ciated entertainment as we passed by onlookers. By the time we arrived, we were all exhausted (well, Harry and I were anyway).

We have the horses in the holding paddock next to the woolshed, and I will keep you posted with our progress. I know Dougal will have a good laugh. Maybe he will even know the horse, given his experience and involvement in the equine world?

As you know, I was a little uncertain about our move here—and I miss you dreadfully, but I am determined to enjoy aspects of our new life. I hope, in time, the place will feel more like home—particularly when I have a proper house and not just a shed to live in!

I had better run now and take this letter down to the wharf to go in the mail bag. Harry is refreshing my driving skills by insisting I drive the truck to Ed's gate. I am a nervous wreck, wrestling with the stupid machine. It's so heavy and hard to steer, and I find it quite frightening. I guess it's a necessary evil, however, so I had better get used to it. We have ordered a Model T Ford which will be marvellous —and hopefully easier for driving in and out to Helensville.

I look forward to hearing from you again soon and send my love and thanks to Catherine for her picture.

Much love to you all,

Alice

CHAPTER 5

"I have no idea why someone would part with that horse?" Harry shook his head as he leaned over the bucket and scrubbed ferociously at the dirt on his arms. "He's a lovely fellow. Seems kind enough under saddle and easy to ride."

Alice looked up. Her floury hands paused on the bread dough. "Still can't guess where he came from?"

"No." He shrugged. "Maybe we'll never know, but whatever his history is, he'll do me very nicely."

She continued kneading as a thread of anxiety wove through her. Like an incoming tide, it surged and receded as she puzzled over the animal's arrival. Was he really a gift? Why had someone addressed him to Harry? Was he some kind of payment—if so, for what? She dearly hoped the whole thing was not a mistake and someone would reclaim him just as they all fell in love with the horse.

"I'll take the boys with me if you like." Harry flicked the towel over his shoulder and picked John up from the highchair. "I'm shifting a load of posts to the back paddock. Hopefully the fences are good enough to move the cattle in there."

"John too?"

"No. Sorry, little man." He nuzzled John's neck and the baby giggled. "I think you need to grow a bit more before I can get you out of Mum's hair."

"Good. In that case, I'll put him in the pram and walk across the flat to the Bennett's. Did you know Mrs Bennett is a schoolteacher and has seven children? I want to meet her and find out what we can do about getting a school built."

"Good idea." He inclined his head before nodding.

She pointed to the batch of biscuits at the end of the table. "I'll take a tin of those with me. With such a big family, I'm sure she'll appreciate them."

"Righto. I'll be off then and see you later." He kissed her on the cheek, plonked John on the floor next to a toy box, then stepped outside and called, "George, Timmy!"

Alice put the bread dough in the large earthenware bowl, covered it with a damp tea towel, and set it to the side of the stove to prove. She shot a glance at John, who was playing happily, then pulled an envelope from her apron pocket, sat at the chair, and reread the letter for the fourth time.

Innisfree
Kingseat
30 November 1935

Dear Alice,

I was delighted to receive your last two letters in yesterday's mail. I must say, I thought the deliveries would be more erratic, but so far, you have been gone a little over a month and I have received four letters from you. Perhaps you're not as isolated as we all thought you'd be?

Alice gazed out the window and her shoulders slumped as she recalled the overheard conversation soon after Harry had purchased Fantail Ridge. It had been between her elder sisters, Mary and Eve, on the occasion of yet another sister, Lily's, wedding.

With their heads bowed and unaware that Alice was partially hidden only yards away, they had shared their opinions.

"Fancy him expecting her to shift way out to the sticks and live like a pioneer when they have everything here at their fingertips," Mary had whispered.

"I think it shows a lack of appreciation for all the things the family do for them," Eve replied.

Alice had frozen at her sister's words. Should she retreat or face them boldly? Her decision had been made for her when one of the catering staff hurried through the door carrying a pile of dirty plates and they almost collided. Plastering a smile on her face, Alice had charged back into the room, walked straight past her siblings, and stopped when she reached the bride.

Lily had reached the ripe old age of thirty-eight, and the family thought she would never marry. She had floored them all when she brought home a tall, thin Australian man, ten years her senior, and introduced him as Godfrey Baxter. Then she'd announced they would be wed before returning to Sale in Victoria, to join his aging parents on the family farm. Alice's family had not just been surprised, they were positively irritated. Where had she met him? *"Certainly not at church"*, James, their eldest brother, had unkindly commented.

Alice didn't care where they had met and, with so few occasions that included them all, had looked forward to Lily's wedding. At least until halfway through the afternoon when, formalities and meal over, guests had begun to waft around the room, catching up with the latest gossip from those they hadn't seen for a while. For Alice, her sisters' whispered conversation had crushed the excitement of their new venture.

She drew a deep breath and returned to the letter.

Dougal has been busy preparing the Clydesdale team for the Christmas parade. He's enlisted both Ken and Hamish's help with washing their legs and brushing them daily. No doubt I will discover my blue-bag missing from the laundry when I wash next time as apparently it makes their feathers as white as snow. Catherine is polishing the harness brasses as I write this and declared this year she will ride in the wagon with her dad and the boys, and I can watch! I will—and I believe employing a man to deal with the milking has been one of the best decisions Dougal ever made.

On a separate note, Father is failing and will miss Lily this Christmas, but Eve, Mary, and I have assured him that he and James will not go hungry. Sid and Eileen will be spending the day with him, and I will give him the Christmas pudding after church next Sunday. Eve made a cake with some of the dried fruit she had stashed away months ago, and Bob said he will dress a chicken for them from his poultry run. Since Lily left, they have been struggling with the domestic side of things, and we were getting a little worried. However, Mary has now employed a plain, but capable young woman called Teresa to cook and clean for them on a daily basis. She lives only a mile away and started work last week. Hopefully that deals with that responsibility.

Have you thought about your children's education? Where will they do their schooling—and how long will you have to live in the shed before you will have a proper house? I am relieved it is you and not me in your situation.

The farmworker is clattering about outside the window now, and I am having difficulty concentrating. So ... I shall finish and find out what he is doing.

I miss you very much and hope you are beginning to settle into your new surroundings? I can't believe that you are driving the truck! You are so brave and make me feel quite inadequate.

My love to you all,

Your loving sister,

Maud

Alice folded the letter again and slid it into the envelope.

"Come on, little fellow. We're going for a walk."

She hoisted John onto her hip, washed his face, and changed him into clean clothes. Then, sitting him on their bed, she tidied her hair, rubbed some cream into her face, and swept a pink lipstick around her mouth. "There, do I look presentable enough to meet my neighbour?" She smiled at John, and he chortled in response.

Lacing up her comfortable leather shoes, she then anchored her wide-brimmed hat on her head with a hat pin and pulled her baby into her arms.

I'll prove to them how wrong they were. Moving to South Head will be the best decision we ever made.

———

WITH JOHN IN THE CANE PRAM AND THE TIN OF BISCUITS tucked under the cover at his feet, she marched out of the gate, across the yard, and began the descent to the swampy flat that led to her neighbour.

The big wheels of the pram ran well on the smooth bits of road, however, the rough gravelled patches and corrugations coming down the hill made for a bumpy ride. Within minutes of leaving home, John was fast asleep.

Arriving at the farm gate, Alice hesitated and

blotted her perspiring face with a handkerchief. A truck blocked the narrow driveway between tall, thick hedges, and she glanced around, seeking other options. *Hmm.* She bulldozed a path with the pram between the truck and the bushy hedge and stepped carefully onto the uneven path. Chooks scratched around the shrubs, and her confidence waned as the closed door in front of her loomed large and imposing.

Before she could turn around and head home again, a door banged somewhere on the other side of the cream painted house, and she jumped.

"Bring that back. It's mine!"

A laugh. A shriek of torment. Then a skinny lad of about ten appeared from the side of the house and ran smack bang into the pram.

"Who are you?" The boy stared at Alice without apology.

"My name is Mrs Simpson, and I am your neighbour." Alice glanced into the pram, relieved to see the jolt had gone unnoticed by the sleeping child. "What's your name?"

"Sam."

A girl arrived and stopped abruptly, her brown eyes growing large as she and Alice studied each other. She wore a pair of boy's shorts and a shirt that, at some point earlier in the day, may have been white. Alice guessed her to be of a similar age to Timmy, her fair hair long and tangled around her tear-stained face.

"Is your mother at home?"

Sam nodded and turned away, grabbing the girl's hand and disappearing around the side of the house.

Presuming his actions meant she should follow, Alice swung the pram in a semi-circle, bouncing it over the paving stones towards the rear of the house.

The back yard was a complete contrast to her own, and Alice stopped abruptly. Her eyes widened. The vast lawn was neatly mowed, edged with garden beds overflowing with flowers of every colour. Shrubs provided a backdrop, while along the roadside fence and protected by a huge hedge, separate beds of vegetables and roses lay in perfectly alignment.

A woman stepped out of the house and onto the veranda, a toddler on her hip. Her height and slim build portrayed a regal appearance—spoiled only by thick brown curls that seemed determined to escape the confines of a bun at the nape of her neck. "Oh, hello. I didn't know you were here." She stared at Alice for a moment before a huge smile spread across her face, and she hurried down the steps. "You must be the new neighbour?"

"I am. Alice Simpson." She nodded at the pram. "And this is my youngest son, John." Alice ran her hand lightly over her hip, suddenly conscious of Irene's willowy physique against her own short, shapely figure.

"How lovely to meet you. I'm so sorry we haven't been up to welcome you …" She glanced around the brood of children that seemed to have popped out of every nook and cranny. "It's a bit hard to get away from this lot." Then she laughed. A deep-throated laugh filled with such joy and amusement that Alice's apprehension melted away, and she smiled in return.

"I'm Irene Bennett. You've just missed my husband, Jack. He and our two eldest have gone to shift cattle. The children love being able to help when there's no school on. Actually, they have to help out all the time, whether it's school or not," she gushed. Reaching out a hand, she clasped Alice's.

"Please come in for a cuppa. It's so nice to have female company, especially one who is going to be living so close."

Alice lifted the waking John from the pram then reached for the tin of biscuits before following Irene inside.

"You have a large family." Alice counted four outside including the toddler. She thought about the two with their father and wondered how on earth this woman coped.

"Seven. Clemmie will be in the bedroom reading, Miles and Bridget are with their dad, and the others are all here. Edith, Sam, Joseph, and little Hugh." She reached her long thin arms out and attempted to gather the remaining children to her. The boy Alice had met on her arrival shrugged himself away from the hug as though embarrassed by the display of affection in front of a visitor. Irene laughed.

"Sam's eleven and thinks he's too big for a hug,

especially in company." She shot a smile at Alice again. "Just wait a few more years and we'll see how he feels."

She pulled out a chair.

"Sit down. I'll put the kettle on, and we'll do our best to have a nice chat without too many distractions."

Alice chuckled as Sam retreated outside once more. With the emergence of a gangly girl Alice assumed was Clemmie, there were five children around the vast dining table, including John. To Alice, the suggestion of a chat without distractions seemed an impossible dream.

CHAPTER 6

Fantail Ridge
South Head
10ᵗʰ December 1935

Dear Maudie,

I hope this finds you all well and happy? Thank you for your last letter—I love hearing your news. I'm enjoying all the Christmas cards that have begun to arrive. They are pinned to the timber framework in this shed-house and cheer the place up immensely. I gave Ed a large bundle to post for me, so hopefully they will be on their way to family and friends by now. He is rather an interesting person, and until now, I had only seen him in the distance. Built like a giant, seems around our age group and yet barely speaks a word! When he does say something, I am sure I detect an accent of some sort, but I can't decide its origin. He lives alone in the shack on the wharf and seems polite, but intensely private. Quite an enigma.

I hope the parade went well last Saturday and that Father is able to enjoy the Christmas food. Hopefully he doesn't get gout like he did last year.

Your question about our children's education prompted me to visit my neighbour, and we have a solution!

Irene and Jack Bennett are our nearest neighbours—only a couple of miles away on the south side of the flat (which I add is mostly swampland that both Bennetts and Harry are attempting to drain).

As a qualified teacher, Irene homeschools her brood of seven children. (Actually, only five are currently school aged, but nevertheless, she is an extraordinary woman.) I felt quite inadequate next to her and came home with new resolutions. In addition to teaching her own family, she has offered to include George and Timmy. She has also studied horticulture and has a huge garden full of vegetables and flowers. I now have a bucket of cuttings from her garden to get me started. They farm cattle and sheep but want to begin a dairy farm and piggery once transporting cream to town becomes possible from our area. At this stage, all cream produced on the peninsula has to be delivered to the factory by boat. With more children moving into the area, Irene is writing to the government to request a proper school out here.

I received a letter from our brother Frank the other day. Of course, being a headmaster, he is also questioning our plans for education, and his letter triggered quite a discussion between Harry and me. The outcome is that we will also advocate in support of Irene's request. Bennetts are offering the education department three and a half acres of their land to have a school built, and Harry believes that if the residents of the peninsula band together, we have a strong case.

You would have laughed if you had been here yesterday. After seeing Irene's garden, I hitched Duke to the plough and we trudged up and down, working a large part of the land we've allocated for vegetable growing. I don't think Duke has ever pulled anything other than the buggy or his racing sulky before, but he was very patient and got the hang of it quite quickly. It was a bit tricky turning at each end, especially as John woke up halfway through.

John has taken his first steps and is already surprisingly quick on his feet, especially when I'm not looking. George and Timmy helped me plant potatoes and kumara, and I also sowed carrots and beans.

The weather is beautiful at the moment—so much so, we are actually hoping for rain. Like most of the country, February is the driest month here, but being between the harbour and the ocean, we seem to get quite a few scuds that are just enough to keep the sandy soil moist.

Irene and Jack have invited us to their place for tea on Christmas Eve. They have a piano, so we can have a good sing-song. My piano has had to take a back seat here lately as I've been busy preserving the plums we bought and making sauce. We found a patch of blackberries on the farm next door (which seems rather wild and unattended), so the boys and I picked a bucketful and I've made jam from them too.

There's a beautifully shaped puriri tree on the top of the hill facing east, and between the shed, the tree, and the road, the land is flat—perfect for our new home, a good-sized lawn, and gardens. Harry made the boys a swing and has hung it from the tree.

As you can probably tell, I am settling in quite well and am sure you will enjoy visiting in due course. I try to make time to have an occasional walk through the bush. It is so soothing, and I love its peace and seeing the pretty native birds. The fantails are my favourite.

I look forward to your next letter and send my love to all,
Your loving sister,
Alice

Alice reread her letter, folded it, and slid it into the addressed envelope. A smile played around her mouth. It was true. When Harry had suggested they move to a completely new district, he had promised her happiness. Reservations and questions had consumed her, and at the time, she fervently doubted that contentment would be possible. She had been wrong.

"Come on, little man. We'll go to see the fantails before your dad and brothers get home." Alice picked up John and reached for her hat.

———

AIDED BY THE SLING OVER HER SHOULDER—FASHIONED from an old flour bag to take the weight of her rapidly growing child—Alice grasped the firmly rooted ferns as she slithered down the bank onto the track.

Each time she walked through the bush, her footprints packed the soil a little more firmly and the path became wider and easier to find. The cool dampness of the overhanging branches and moss clinging to the dripping bank greeted Alice. A fantail twittered in front of her, flitting from one side of the track to the other as though inviting her to follow. John lifted a chubby hand and pointed, chortling, his attempts at one-syllable words loud and excitable.

She held her finger up to her closed lips. "Shh. We want the birds to be our friends, and if you make too much noise, you'll frighten them away."

Alice stopped regularly, pointing out the bush creatures to John as she made her way towards the foot of the hill: a tui with its white tuft of feathers under his chin, a weta scuttling across the track in front of them before disappearing under a rotting log, and a kereru flapping briefly above them, almost hidden amongst the fronds of the huge tree fern. And all the time, the fantails chattered and dived left and right, catching insects on the wing with their dainty little beaks, the white feathers above their eyes providing them with a slightly worried appearance.

The bush opened out onto a flat area of grass at the bottom of the steep slope, and Alice stopped, her eyes following the rise to the top. A triangular section of rough grasses ran between the road and the bush, its widest point meeting the flat section of ground that was to become the lawns and gardens around her new home.

She repositioned John on her hip and bent her head towards his, pointing her finger to the rough slope. "That's going to be my special project. I'm going to fill it with beautiful trees and lots of daffodils, so that when I'm old and you're a grown man, I can sit at the top and watch the birds and bees—and remember what it was like when we came here."

John gabbled unintelligibly and grinned. Alice drew a deep breath and began trudging towards the top of the hill.

Reaching the summit, she paused again, red faced and panting. She turned a slow circle, savouring the views in every direction, and expelled a long, contented breath.

In the distance, the figure of a man dressed in khaki appeared from behind the woolshed, immediately followed by two children in baggy shorts and bare feet. Accompanying them was a sandy coloured dog with its tail in the air.

Alice smiled and allowed John to slither to the ground. Taking him by the hand and walking at a snail's pace, they made their way towards her approaching family.

———

"C AN WE FIND A C HRISTMAS TREE?" G EORGE ASKED breathlessly.

Harry wrinkled his forehead then grinned and lay a hand on George's shoulder. "Of course. We'll see if we can find a small pine tree and put it in the corner of the shed. You boys can help Mum decorate it tomorrow." Harry looked at Alice and they shared a smile.

Warmth spread through her like a blanket—soft and comforting. Her boys had been working hard, proving themselves as competent as many twice their age, and her chest swelled with pride. *Tonight, after you've gone to sleep, I'll light a second kerosene lamp and finish sewing the new shorts and shirts for you all.* Together with the book and a small packet of jellybeans she had bought for each of them, the clothes would brighten up their day when they woke and emptied their Christmas stockings.

Excitement filtered through the family, and Timmy jumped up and down. "And can we make decorations? And shortbread?"

"We'll make the decorations tomorrow once the tree is in place, then we'll do some cooking next week," Alice said.

"I wish we could have Christmas with Ken and Hamish," George said quietly.

Alice rested her hand gently on her son's arm. "I know. We all do. But we talked about this. We can't go this year, but we'll see them next Christmas."

George nodded silently and scuffed the ground.

"This year we're getting to know new friends. Our neighbours. Then, in February, you and Timmy are going to the Bennett house each day to join their children in the classroom," Alice said.

"A classroom?" Timmy almost shouted in horror. "I don't need to go to school."

"Don't be stupid, Timmy. Everybody has to go to school. How else do you think you'll learn to read and write?" George turned to his brother and scowled.

"I don't need to read and write." Timmy folded his arms across his chest and stuck his bottom lip out.

"Oh dear. And here I was thinking what grown-up young men I was working with," Harry said.

Alice rolled her eyes.

"Your Dad's right, Timmy. You said when you grow up you want to work on trucks and cars and learn how engines work. Just imagine if you couldn't read any information about them. How would you know what to do? School is important, and you're very lucky that Mrs Bennett has offered to teach you."

Timmy huffed and silently kicked the dirt.

Harry winked at Alice and glanced across the estuary. "The barge is coming in shortly, and I reckon our cow and her new calf should be onboard. We'll go down to the wharf so we can be ready to get her off and bring her home."

"That will be wonderful," Alice said. "Can you wait a minute while I fetch my letter to Maud?"

"Of course. Where is it? George can get it for you."

"It's on the table, George. You can't miss it." The boy sped off while Harry and Alice stood side by side and gazed across the farm to the harbour. He was back within a couple of minutes, and Harry tucked the letter into his shirt pocket. "Coming, boys?"

The schooling issue was forgotten as both George and Timmy raced to the top of the road, where only a few minutes earlier, Alice had stood.

"I'd say that's a yes." Harry smiled at Alice and bent to pat the dog. "We won't take Rock. It's best to walk the cattle home slowly, and we know how upset cows get when there's a dog around their new calf."

He stepped forward and gave Alice a peck on the cheek.

"Perhaps you would open the gate in about an hour? We'll leave them to settle in tonight and then tomorrow can begin our new routine."

"I will. I'm looking forward to having fresh milk and butter. Come on, Rock. You can watch John for me while I peel the veggies."

The dog hesitated, waiting until his master's hat disappeared over the crown of the hill, then he turned and trotted dutifully after Alice, his head low and his pink tongue lolling.

CHAPTER 7

A week later, Alice sat on the tiny three-legged stool, her head leaning gently on the jersey cow's flank as the milk flowed rhythmically into the bucket. They had called her Josie, for no other reason than they agreed it was a nice name. Although a little flighty to begin with, the cow had quickly adjusted to her new home. She stood patiently while Button, her calf, sucked the two teats on her left side and Alice milked as fast as she could on the right. The boys had named the tiny bull calf following the discovery of two vertical white spots on his honey-coloured chest, perfectly formed and identical, resembling fastenings on a vest.

"Mail, Mum." George flapped a letter as he ran towards her, startling the cow. Josie kicked out, narrowly missing both the bucket and Alice's leg.

"Stop! George, you must remember she's not used to children or things being waved close to her."

Harry closed the gate and followed the boys while Alice clutched the bucket and soothed the agitated cow. She had been relieved when he offered to take the children with him to meet the boat, allowing her and Josie to become more acquainted.

"Another pile of mail—and guess what." He held a small red box with a picture of grapes on the outside and smiled. "Raisins."

"Really? That's wonderful. Where did you get them from?"

"Ed. I asked him the day I bought the mullet net and he said he'd see what he could do. Sometimes, it seems, it's all about contacts."

Alice returned the smile and picked up the bucket. Releasing the chain from behind the cow, she patted her on the rump. "Good girl. You can back up now."

While Josie took her time to move, Alice handed Harry the milk pail, took John by the hand, and the little family slowly made their way to the shed.

She stirred up the embers and added wood to the fire before filling the kettle and sitting it on the stove. Then she sat and opened the envelope addressed in Maud's elegant writing.

Innisfree

Kingseat

12 December 1935

Dearest Alice,

I hope all is well and settled by now and I didn't sound condescending when I congratulated you for writing four letters in such a short time. What I meant was that I thought it wonderful that, in spite of your relative isolation, the mail system seems to be quite efficient. I haven't forgotten that one of our promises to each other was to not be as free with criticism as some of our siblings tend to be. You and I need each other's support, no matter what is thrown in our direction.

A warmth coursed through Alice, and she lowered the letter to her lap. Even though Maud did not always keep her opinions to herself, where Alice was concerned, they were well meant, and Alice had long ago accepted that it was just Maud's way. She read on.

I expect our mail will be crossing each week—so I am answering your letter of 3rd December.

Helensville sounds like a nice little town—and I am relieved to hear you received your piano, horse, and buggy without too many incidents. Odd about the unexpected horse. Dougal was quite miffed when I told him and said he would make some enquiries about it. I find your confidence with horses amazing, and I wish I shared even a smidgeon of it. Just my luck to have married a man who loves and values horses as much as he does me (at least that's how it feels sometimes!). The huge creatures that fill our paddocks still frighten the living daylights out of me in spite of being constantly reminded that Clydesdales are 'the gentle giants of the horse world'.

The Christmas parade went off well—no rain, and even I

could appreciate how magnificent the horses looked. Catherine was as proud as punch sitting up in the wagon next to her father and told me she waved to everyone like the royal princesses do. I'm not sure where she would have seen that—from a picture book perhaps?

I received a letter this week from Lily. She asked for your address, so perhaps you will find time to write to her? She is having a baby—so there you are! Thirty-nine is not too old, after all. Although I suspect she may find her life changes considerably more than she expects. Reading between the lines, I think she is feeling the distance between us, although assures me that her mother-in-law is very kind and helpful. I get the impression she is also a little possessive of her only son though, but that's to be expected.

I heard via the grape vine that Paddy has not enjoyed staying on your old farm with the new owners. Evidently, they are quite officious and treat him like a slave. After finishing the two weeks he promised, he moved on to Robert's farm. You never told me he is a prolific reader. I got a surprise when he came to help Dougal start a couple of the young Clydesdales in harness and had a book called Lonely Road *by Neville Shute in his bag. He offered it to Dougal to read, but you know Dougal—except for the newspaper, the only books he ever studies are about horses in some form or another!*

The hydrangeas are all out in bloom now and are quite a show in the driveway. I hope your cuttings strike in that sandy soil and give you as much pleasure as mine give me. I took a bunch to church last Sunday and put some on Emmie's grave then gave the rest to the Vicar's wife. It won't be long before the dahlia's are flowering, so I will take them in due course. It does brighten up the cemetery, and I am sure that if Emmie was with us now, she would love flowers as much as Catherine does. (And of course as much as you and I do too).

I really don't have much other news from here. I've had trouble getting dried fruit and other little extras this year to make Christmas special. Hopefully the economy will improve soon and this wretched depression ends. On the positive side, we have to be thankful we live on a farm. At least we have fresh food!

I look forward to your next letter.

My love to you all,

Maud

A gamut of emotions swept through Alice. Pleasure at receiving Maud's letter was mixed with compassion for Lily and a revelation about herself. She didn't cry—or even think she might—at the mention of Emmie. Perhaps leaving her tiny body so far away would not be as hard as she had expected? Her daughter's soul, the memory of her scent and her smile would always remain with Alice. If she listened hard enough, she could still hear the echo of Emmie's first chuckle. This time Maud's mention of her brought gratitude.

"I thought we might try our hands at catching mullet," Harry said.

Alice blinked. With her mind still on Emmie, it took a moment to register what Harry was saying. "When?"

Harry smiled. "Now. The tide's coming in, and I'm keen to see how we go casting the net."

Alice raised her eyebrows. Harry's suggestion was a practical one, even if hauling a mullet net around in thigh-deep water didn't appeal quite as much to her as it did to him. However, her concern for her husband was growing, and she was pleased that he wanted to take a break from the farm. He had barely stopped since they arrived on Fantail Ridge and was now almost as thin as he had been on his post-war return from Egypt. In the evenings, he managed only to bath, eat his meal, and help wash up before he fell asleep in the chair.

It took a few minutes to gather towels and hats for them all, and to collect the spare buckets from the wash house. The air in the truck filled with excitement as the children clambered in, bouncing and chattering with delight. Alice allowed herself to relax in quiet anticipation.

While Timmy and John played in the small patch of sand below the grassy bank, Harry waded into the incoming tide, his hands full of what appeared to be a tousled mesh of rope. As he called instructions, the net slowly unravelled, and the unwieldy tangle sank into the water.

"You and George hang on to it tight and stay where

you are. George, take the lower end and let Mum hang on to the top. I'll circle out a bit deeper then come back towards you." Harry's voice carried across the gently lapping waves as they rhythmically crept closer.

"It's quite heavy." Alice was shocked. New respect bloomed for the fisherman in the Manukau Harbour she had watched growing up, throwing their nets across the water as though they were made of feathers.

Within minutes, they were hauling the sodden bundle towards the bank, where the grass ended and mangroves took over. Fish flapped and gasped their final breath.

"Timmy! The buckets," Alice called. Mud squelched between her toes, and she shuddered. The cool water swirling around her ankles was soothing as long as firm sand remained under her feet, but no matter how hard she breathed and pretended she was standing on a bed of down, she could not adjust to the soft, sticky depths of the muddy unknown.

The boys helped Harry untangle and count their catch.

"Eight mullet, Mum." George's usual solemn demeanour morphed to exhilaration, and his eyes widened as he counted them again.

"Well … I know what we're eating for tea tonight," Alice said. She reached for John's hand. He clung silently to her skirt, as though trying to understand why his father and brothers were so jubilant over such peculiar creatures. She squatted down and hugged him tightly.

The warmth had gone from the sun, and its shimmering rays bubbled on the harbour as it slipped slowly behind the hills to the west.

While Harry rolled up the net, Alice was surprised to see Ed appear from behind the headland, skimming towards them in a dingy. The oars bumped in the rowlocks as he approached, and he raised them out of the water before leaping from the boat and dragging the bow to a halt in the sand.

"We're having fish for tea," Timmy announced.

Ed nodded and inspected the catch. "I can smoke some for you?"

"Thanks, Ed. We'd appreciate that. We haven't got our smoke house built yet," Harry said.

"Nor has our fridge arrived, but hopefully that is not far away now." Alice smiled at the man, taking in his ragged shorts and threadbare shirt. His eyes were a deep blue, similar to Harry's, and his skin as tanned. There, the similarity stopped. Tall and well built, he towered over her husband, and she had to tear her gaze from his huge hands. Not for the first time, she wondered what had kept him hunkered alone in a tiny hut for so many years. Perhaps Irene would know more about him. She would ask.

With the net stowed next to the fish on the back of the truck, she lifted John onto the seat and stood back while the other boys clambered into the cab. Harry started the engine while Alice watched the solitary soul push the dingy out and leap lightly into the tiny vessel. The truck turned away from the beach, and Alice glanced back. The fading light touched the water, silhouetting Ed as he rowed the dingy into the distance. It was an image that burned into her mind. *Is solitude his choice?*

CHAPTER 8

Fantail Ridge
South Head
26 December 1935

Dear Maudie,

It's hard to comprehend that Christmas is over and we have lived here for two months already. I hope you enjoyed the festivities and company and are now able to rest a little before the show season begins.

We went to the Bennett's for dinner as planned. Irene and I took turns playing the piano while we sang carols and Christmas hymns etc. We had roast goose—very nice. It was from the flock that seems to wander on their side of the swampy flat. I took some of the smoked mullet that Ed did for us and one of the puddings that I made last week. I know it should have been made weeks ago, but it tasted good and there wasn't a crumb left. I also asked Irene if she knows anything about Ed's history, but she didn't.

Anyway, when we returned home (in the dark), we received a wonderful surprise. A man was sitting on the step outside the boys' bedroom. I got quite a start until I realised it was Paddy! Can you believe it? He caught the train to the railhead in Helensville, then waited until he could get a lift on someone's truck. They took him to Mairetahi, and he walked from there to our place. I gave the poor man food and a hot drink, and we eventually settled everyone into bed. We dusted off an old mattress from the loft in the shed and made a bed for Paddy on the floor up there. He assured us he was quite comfortable. I hope the possum that we have not yet been able to evict doesn't bother him too much!

We had invited the two bachelors from nearby farms (Vince and Clive) and also Ed, who declined (very politely), to join us for lunch on Christmas Day. Everyone enjoyed the roast mutton and vegetables, and the pudding went down well! I put two three-pences in it and was pleased when George's piece held one of them. Vince got the other one, but he kindly gave it to Timmy. The men stayed until nearly dark, talking and laughing with us and playing cricket out on the lawn with the boys. So, all in all, everyone had a wonderful day.

I wonder what 1936 will bring. We hope for a good year —and with Paddy here now to help out, it has a great beginning. If the economy improves and everyone remains in good health, it will be enough for me.

We've received a pile of letters and cards from family and friends for Christmas. Before I put them away, I will reread them all and respond as soon as I can. James' letter included reminders of how grateful I should be to Eve and Mary for stepping in and taking care of Father and him. I'm not sure when or if he will ever accept that I have my own life with my husband and family. Do you still get cross with him when he nags you? He didn't mention you at all, so I suspect there may have been a few words spoken—am I right?

I am surrounded by men here, however, they're all so much more appreciative of my cooking than our brother and father ever have been, so I really don't mind. Irene is not far away, and although I haven't used the telephone for social reasons, I know it is there if I want or need to.

The new kerosene fridge has arrived and is wonderful. Also, having the cow is a blessing as we were all getting a bit sick of powdered milk and dripping.

Perhaps next Christmas you will all be able to come and stay for a few days here instead of us going to you? We'll be better organised by then and can purchase one of those canvas tents that are becoming more common—or perhaps our proper house will have been built? I live in hope.

We're hoping the weather will hold for a bit longer so we can get the hay made. We actually need rain, but if we can get at least some of it cut and baled before it arrives, we'll be happy. The baler we bought is old and a bit cantankerous, but we're lucky we managed to get one at all. The grasses here are different and much more varied to those at Karaka, so we hope they make good hay. I had visions of having to drive Duke around the paddocks towing the baler—and maybe I still will! It all sounds a bit overwhelming, but no doubt we will cope. Now that John is running everywhere, I need three pairs of hands.

I hope all are well and happy, and I look forward to receiving your report on Christmas and family soon.

With much love to you all,

Alice

Alice put the lid on her fountain pen and blotted the page. Before folding it, she reread what she had written and satisfied she had covered all matters that would interest Maud, she addressed the envelope, inserted the letter, and propped it against the vase of flowers in the centre of the table.

"Do you want to come and have a look at our handiwork?" Harry popped his head through the open window and wiped his forehead on his shirt sleeve.

"I would love to. What have you and your trusty assistants been up to this time?"

Harry smiled and tucked Alice's hand through the crook of his arm. "You'll see. Put your hat on because we've got a little way to go."

Alice's interest piqued. "Where's John?"

"Don't worry. He's safe with Paddy and the boys. He fell asleep, so we achieved more than we thought."

Alice lengthened her stride in step with her husband. They crossed the lane in front of the shed and headed down the slope towards the woolshed. As they neared the building, Timmy ran to them, grabbing Alice's free hand and urging her to hurry.

Expecting to step over the footing at the bottom of the side door, she was surprised when the boys led her around behind the building. A tiny wooden hut stood at the end of the spider's web of yards. She gathered her skirt before negotiating the block of wood that served as a step and stood in the doorway. Her nostrils flared at the scent of lanolin and sheep manure, and sunlight poured through the open angled window, illuminating dust particles in the air.

"What do you think?" George asked.

The empty wool bales, boxes of assorted steel and leather, and the network of cobwebs that had previously overflowed the building had been replaced with an old iron bed. Resting on the wire mesh, a horsehair mattress lay, covered in black and white striped canvas.

"This is Paddy's bedroom—for the moment anyway," Timmy burst out, unable to contain himself.

"Oh, Paddy, it's a … a bit primitive and small."

"Mrs Alice. It will do me fine. Any road, it's only temporary. Once your house has been built, there will be other options, and until then, I will be comfortable here." Paddy grinned widely, showing gaps where teeth should have been.

"But what about a toilet—and somewhere to wash?"

"All taken care of," Harry said. Taking Alice's hand, he led her to the window overlooking the gentle slope that ran down to the gully. "We've moved the outhouse and dug a new hole. That will serve perfectly well for the moment. The water tank is full, and the hand basin in the woolshed functions adequately."

Paddy was a valuable worker, and Alice cringed at the thought that he might not have been happy in the loft. Was it too dirty? Were they too noisy for him? While doubts swept through her mind, she started as Paddy touched her arm.

"I like it here. It gives us all our privacy, and I can set up my books over there." He pointed to two slabs of wood resting on empty kerosene tins to form a set of bookshelves. With an upturned fruit box serving as a bedside table, Paddy appeared delighted with his new accommodation.

"We'll give him our spare lamp and blankets and all that kind of stuff." Harry beamed, clearly delighted with their afternoon's activities. "And he'll still come up to the house for his bath and meals."

Alice relaxed. If that's all it took to please him, then who was she to question it? Eve's voice rankled in the back of her mind. *Don't trust him. He's not only Irish, he's a Catholic, and you're quite mad to allow him on your property.*" Alice had been not only shocked, but furious at her sister's attitude. She had bitten her tongue until it bled, containing her silent retort. *Just because your husband's a supporter of the Orange Order in Belfast and has managed to brainwash you, you've no right to judge this kind and helpful little man.*

"I'll fetch the bed linen and blankets from the loft if that's alright with you, Mrs Alice?"

"Of course it is, Paddy." She turned and smiled at the children. "You've all done a wonderful job. Now, who would like a drink and a piece of Christmas cake?"

"Me!" Both boys chorused, waking John.

As they trailed back up the paddock towards the house, Harry rested his arm across Alice's shoulders. "What do you think? It's been a pretty good start to our new life so far, hasn't it?"

She smiled and kissed his cheek. "It certainly has."

CHAPTER 9

Fantail Ridge, May 1938

THE DAY DAWNED CRISP AND CLEAR, AND ALICE breathed a sigh of relief. After weeks of blustery showers that drove almost horizontally across the land, she was beginning to wonder how much longer they would have to put off shearing. In preparation for the event, she and the boys had mustered their flocks while Harry and Paddy each took a shearing stand, deftly removing the dirty wool from around each sheep's rear end. Their combined effort in between the showers had ensured the pre-shearing crutch on the long Romney wool was completed in plenty of time.

However, if the rain continued and they couldn't get them shorn soon, winter would be upon them. Alice shuddered at the thought of the poor sheep having to withstand cold westerly winds with no wool for protection and wasn't at all sure that this plan to shear twice a year was a good one.

Harry reached up and turned on the radio. It crackled for a few seconds before the voice sounded through the airwaves, deep and clear. Alice stood next to her husband, listening intently as the weather report began.

"A high has settled over the North Island, bringing with it a period of warm, dry air. This is expected to remain for at least a week ..." Static buzzing replaced the smooth, serious tones of the radio announcer, and Harry fiddled with the knobs. It took only seconds to regain clarity by which time the forecast was over.

"Well, it sounds as though we should be right for a while." Harry's face lit up, and he rubbed his hands together before stoking the wood fire. "I'll ring Bill and see how soon he and his boys can come."

Apprehension filled Alice. The shearers had been scheduled to come two weeks ago and were delayed due to the weather, meaning there was a good chance the Fantail Ridge sheep had gone to the bottom of the queue.

A knock sounded on the back door, and Paddy popped his head inside. "Here's the milk, Mrs Alice."

"Thank you, Paddy. Come in and sit down. The boys are still asleep, and the builders haven't appeared yet either."

She put a cup of tea in front of him and turned back to listen to Harry's telephone conversation.

"Yes, tomorrow would be fine if that suits you. We'll be ready." Harry's confident tone belied the look he shot Alice as he spoke.

Her eyes opened wide, and she held out her upturned hands. "Tomorrow?" she whispered.

"Thanks, Bill. We'll see you in the morning. Goodbye." He hung up the receiver and grimaced at Alice and Paddy. "Sorry, folks. It was either tomorrow or wait another month until they're available again—and I don't want to do that."

Alice took a deep breath and gathered her thoughts as Harry continued.

"So—we have the contractor and four shearers arriving tomorrow. No presser or shed hands, and it's only due to your cooking that they're coming. Have you got enough stores to feed everyone, Alice?"

"Yes. If you can dress another mutton for me, we'll have plenty. I'll ring an order through to the grocer and see if they can send it out on the boat and drop it at Ed's store." She paused for a moment and gazed around the room. "Where are we going to put everyone this time?"

Construction had finally begun on the new house the week after Easter. The framework was up, but progress had been slow due to the rain, and the sheets of roofing iron still lay under canvas on the lawn.

Voices outside signalled visitors approaching, and Harry opened the door, startling the two men.

"Come in, boys. We've got a bit to discuss." He stepped to the side and gestured for them to sit down. The two builders were cousins, one a few years older than the other, but with a family likeness that was undeniable. Both wore overalls, thick cotton shirts, and their smooth, brown complexions spoke of many hours in the sun.

Alice placed the bread on the table and spooned porridge into the row of bowls. She met the pairs of deep brown eyes with her own grey-blue ones. "Please start. I'm going to get the boys before this goes cold." She darted through the door dividing the living quarters from the shed and climbed halfway up the ladder.

The loft had been scrubbed and lined with plywood the previous winter, offering a cold but spacious room for extras to sleep in until the house was built. With the arrival of the builders, the boys had happily relocated upstairs, allowing the men to use the room on the side of the shed. And, at almost four, John had insisted he was big enough to be included. Alice and Harry relished the fact that, after ten years, they finally had a bedroom to themselves.

"Come on, boys. Get dressed and come to breakfast. The shearers are coming tomorrow, and we've got lots to do."

George was reading, snuggled under the eiderdown. He threw it back and sat up at his mother's voice. "Dad will need my help."

"And mine," Timmy echoed, his voice muffled and half-hearted, as though he didn't want to be left out but wasn't awake enough to cooperate.

John remained fast asleep, and Alice continued climbing up the ladder and stroked his face. "Wake up, little man. Time to get up."

———

SHE CLOSED THE OVEN DOOR AND WIPED THE perspiration from her forehead. "Two loaves of bread, scones, and a batch of biscuits done, casserole and cake in the oven. Now, what's next?" Alice muttered to herself and squared her shoulders.

Having sent the boys with Harry to begin mustering, she had a limited window of child-free time to achieve as much as possible. The sheets were flapping on the line, the water in the copper cooling before she could bucket it out onto the garden. She glanced at the clock, grabbed her writing pad and pen, and began.

Fantail Ridge
South Head
15 May 1938

Dear Maud,
Apologies for this being a very hurried letter, but the

shearers are coming tomorrow, and I have so much to do my head is spinning! We've been waiting for the rain to stop and now the sun is out—hence the short notice. The contractor (Bill) is bringing four men, so my kitchen has turned into a bakery and Harry has a half-crippled man and a pint-sized team of under ten-year-olds to help him! Thank goodness it's school holidays. George and Timmy are mustering on their horses (Duke has accepted the saddle at last and is surprisingly good with George, so Timmy now rides Stormy). Harry and John are in the truck, supervising the workforce, opening gates, and directing Rock—actually, the dog is probably doing most of the work.

Paddy has a sore hip and said he would rather not ride a horse (I had a giggle to myself as the way he said it sounded like he would prefer to ride a cow or a camel). Instead he made a rattle out of an old treacle tin (a wire handle, a few stones inside, and the lid clamped on tight) and says that's all he needs. He'll look after the yards and keep the pens full. One positive is everyone will sleep well!

I picked the last of the peas yesterday and have planted broad beans. While I am stuck inside cooking, I'm listening to the radio (we love it). Isn't Aunt Daisy great? The way she begins her broadcast "Good morning, good morning, good morning everybody" makes me feel so included. I've been writing down the recipes she shares too and trying them out on the family. By tomorrow there will be nine men to feed, plus three boys, so I had better get back to it all now and take this down to Ed before dark.

I'll write again when shearing is over.

Lots of love to you all,
Alice

———

IT WAS MID-AFTERNOON, AND A STRONG BREEZE BLEW IN from the east. Alice picked up the wicker laundry basket and shoved her feet into her gumboots. Josie grazed nonchalantly amongst the dandelions and lush green grass a few yards from the flapping washing, and she raised her head, her jaw grinding from side to side as she chewed her cud, seemingly interested in Alice's approach.

"Nothing for you today, girl. Just retrieving these and then you can have the paddock to yourself again."

Alice lowered the prop just enough to reach the pegs without the sheets touching the grass or, worse still, the cow pats dotted across the paddock. Then, with the basket piled high, she lugged it back to the shed and kicked off her boots. With the linen sorted and slung over her shoulders, she climbed the ladder to the loft and remade the boys' beds before moving out into the men's room to prepare it for another invasion of testosterone. As she tucked in the last sheet and plumped the final pillow, she glanced out the window to her new house.

The roof cladding was being passed from one builder to the other, and progress appeared to have stepped up a notch. She grinned. There was nothing like having nowhere else to sleep to encourage an increase in pace. Unless they roofed the house today, they would be camping beneath the stars. Two camp stretchers leaned against an internal wall frame, and Alice picked up a pile of spare blankets and two pillows. It was only for a week, and if they got the roof on and lined a few walls, they would have privacy and shelter before the shearers finished. She would even make their beds up for them.

AN HOUR LATER, ALICE CAUTIOUSLY REVERSED THE Model T Ford out of its shed and turned to face the road. With her letter to Maud on the seat next to her, she drove towards the wharf, delighted with her successful negotiation of the entrance at the bottom of the hill. She had doubts she would ever be a confident driver but, with no other traffic to consider, a satisfied smile spread across her face in the knowledge she could at least do something none of her sisters had even attempted.

Ed was not at the store or around the back in his garden. She studied the neat rows of turnips for a minute, wondering why he needed so many. Were they his staple diet? Potatoes and a kumara patch had been fenced off behind the hut, adding some variation to the root vegetable, but there was no sign of any peas or cabbages she had discovered grew so well on the peninsula.

A movement caught her eye, and she peered at the water shimmering in the late afternoon light. An oar was raised, possibly in acknowledgement of her presence and she assumed it to be Ed. She waved and flapped the white envelope, pointing as she lay it on the wooden table outside the shack. Moving the rock that rested on the tabletop, she pinned the letter down and swung her gaze back to the harbour. Even though he was a hundred yards away, the occupant of the boat made no attempt to row towards her.

She waited for a moment before giving another cheery wave and returning to the car.

I've been coming down for over two years now and can count on my hand the number of words he has spoken to me. Perhaps he is an escaped criminal and doesn't want to be caught? She laughed.

CHAPTER 10

For days, the skies remained clear, the breeze gentle, and the residents of Fantail Ridge, exhausted but joyous. The woolshed floor was stacked high with large square hessian bales, each tightly packed with the long, lustrous wool of the Romneys. The packs would have to sit there until Harry could transport them to the harbour barge for delivery to the Auckland Wool Stores. Meanwhile, every sheep on the property was sent through the plunge dip, a long narrow bath filled with foul-smelling liquid designed to eradicate each and every louse that may or may not attempt to make a home in the warm, moist wool. Each sheep received a health check and had its hooves trimmed if necessary before they were divided into separate mobs and returned to fresh paddocks, this time joined by the rams. If everything went to plan, this year's lambs would begin to arrive in late October—in perfect time to enjoy spring, warmer weather, and good feed.

Too tired to do more than essential chores, Harry suggested they take a picnic to the beach. Paddy and the builders joined in, pleased to have a break. With them providing sufficient manpower in dragging the net, Alice relaxed on the rug, revelling in the sun soaking through her jacket and warming her back. The men built a fire on the small patch of sand a few yards from the mangroves and surrounded it with rocks, then set the billy over the flames to boil.

While everyone sipped the hot dark liquid, Harry lay the freshly scaled and gutted fish on the blackened steel plate inches above the fire and nestled the cast-iron pot of potatoes in the remaining hot coals. Alice drizzled butter and lemon juice over the mullet, leaping back as it dripped onto the hot steel and spat drips into the air.

"My mouth is watering," Paddy announced and moved closer to the fire.

When they had eaten their fill, Harry reheated the billy, and Alice opened a cake tin, revealing the last of the little apple tarts she had made the previous day.

It was a replete but satisfied straggle of adults and children who made their way back to the truck as darkness fell. The temperature was dropping quickly, and raindrops appeared from nowhere, bouncing off the windscreen. Those piled on the back of the vehicle pulled a tarpaulin over their heads and huddled together. Winter was on its way.

———

Fantail Ridge
South Head
28 May 1938

DEAR MAUD,

Hello again. How are you? I haven't received any mail for two weeks now but guess I will receive a bundle very soon! There is talk of the cream lorry run being extended as butter prices are rising and the Kaipara Dairy is encouraging farmers to expand. Once that happens, we will receive mail regularly and more often.

Shearing is over for another six months—yes, they'll be back again in summer due to the increasing demand for fat lambs. Our flock has grown to almost two thousand now. Growing such long fleeces, (after six months, their wool is as long as most other breeds are in twelve), Romneys health can be better managed in this climate if shorn twice a year. The shearing team were nice men, and I was quite chuffed at the compliments I received for my cooking. It would seem the meals on some properties are not very good. We were all tired by the time we waved them goodbye, and I'm pleased I can use up leftovers for a couple of days before I have to get back into my routine again.

We had a stroke of good luck—not only with the weather,

but also with the engine that runs the shearing plant. It sent out a cloud of smoke during the final run of sheep and then stopped altogether. No one could find the problem, so the shearers had to sharpen their blades and finish the last hundred sheep using hand shears. Although slower, they did a great job, and everyone heaved a huge sigh of relief. Now Harry has to see if he can find the problem—and then work out how to fix it!

I will miss George and Timmy next week when they return to school, but the builders are progressing well with our house, so I hope to get into town and have a look at curtain material and suchlike.

The best news ever is that our new school is also under construction. Apparently, with winter close at hand, someone must have felt guilty about the children having to sit in a canvas marquee for hours while the wind blew through it. Irene will step back from her role as a new teacher has been appointed by the education board. He's bringing a caravan to live in. All very exciting—South Head is progressing! They are even changing the name of the school from Mairetahi to Waioneke.

Although our days are busy, we are getting to know our neighbours better and enjoy the occasional social gatherings that have begun to take place. Next weekend, we have been invited to a bonfire and 'pot-luck' meal (where we all take a pot of food to share) at a woolshed about ten miles farther up the peninsula. We haven't had much time to explore that area or meet the new residents yet, so I'm looking forward to it.

The builders have set up camp in what will be our boys' bedroom in the new house. I'm relieved as the men's room attached to this shed is much warmer than the loft for our children, and I will no longer have to climb up and down the ladder.

Paddy has asked me to visit the library next time I am in town. Apparently, there is an author called Agatha Christie, and he's keen to read her books. Have you heard of her? He's such a strange man at times (Paddy, I mean). So polite and private, but obviously his imagination receives plenty of stimulation from the amount of reading he does. The other day he asked me if I had been to see where Vince is domiciled. His old-fashioned expression took me by surprise. (By the way, no I haven't). Paddy's been helping Harry drag the mullet net but won't go to town and says he hates boats. George told us that Paddy came to New Zealand on a boat when he was George's age—so maybe he was a cabin boy or something and developed a fear of the sea, or ships, or both? It appears we may discover more about his past through the children—am I being too nosey? I don't think so. I'm just interested in people and the history that makes them who they are.

I look forward to hearing all your news and send our love to you all,

Your loving sister,

Alice

———

With the exception of the rain the night of their fish picnic, the weather had remained surprisingly mild for several days before the temperature plummeted, driving the family closer to the fire at night. A golden hue in late afternoon and the autumn colours of the trees brought with them a softness to the peninsula, and Alice loved it.

The following week, she was agitating the butter churn in the storeroom, her face flushed with exertion when Timmy's voice shrilled through the timber walls.

"Mum, where are you?"

Alice poked her head out the open door. "In here."

It was Saturday, and George and Timmy had been sent to check on the newly shorn sheep while Harry took the malfunctioning shearing engine to Ed's store. He had poured over a manual filled with tiny writing for days and fiddled with the contraption in the shed, eventually giving up, deciding instead to send the whole apparatus into town for repair.

"We found a dog." George stumbled into sight half-carrying, half-dragging a huge, filthy looking creature, which he lowered onto the ground at Alice's feet. It's sunken eyes were dark and mournful, and its painfully thin body lay like a sack full of bones.

She wiped her hands on her apron and knelt beside the animal as its tail thumped weakly on the ground. "Oh you poor thing." Alice looked up at the boys. "Where did you find him?" Alice lifted one of the dogs hind legs gently and lowered it again. "Her. She's a girl dog."

"In the back paddock, near the ridge that goes through the bush to the coast." George crouched next to the dog and stroked her head.

"We thought it was a wild creature of some sort to begin with," Timmy added. "We rode away from her, but she looked so sad, so we slowed down, and she followed us all the way home." He shrugged and raised upturned hands.

John had been sitting on the concrete outside the shed, attempting to hammer nails into a block of wood with a home-forged tool that required both hands to control it—and even then, the little boy was too small to have much effect. He abandoned his project hurriedly and wrapped his arms around the dog's neck. "Can we keep her, Mum?"

"We don't know anything about her. She must belong to someone. Perhaps she got lost or left behind and her owner has been searching for her." Alice attempted to reason with the boys. "She needs a bath and something to eat before we make any decisions."

The boys needed no further encouragement and dashed into the wash house, dragging the tin tub into the sunshine minutes later. Running back and forth with buckets, they partly filled the bath, and Alice added a stream of boiling water from the kitchen kettle. She rolled up her sleeves, and together, they lifted the dog into the water and scrubbed her gently with laundry soap. Her skinny body shook, and she whimpered while her face remained stiff with misery. When the washing was over, she refused to get out of the tub, and the four of them were soaked by the time they had lifted her onto the grass. They rubbed her with clean rags, and just as they stepped back to admire their handiwork, she let out a sorrowful howl—something akin to that of a wolf or a bloodhound—and once again collapsed in a heap.

Alice was sure she could hear her bones rattle, and her heart ached. Mostly black, the dog's legs, chest, and part of her face were highlighted in a bright coppery-tan colour. The tip of her tail was white—together with a few small splashes on one paw.

"She's quite good looking, isn't she?" Timmy said.

Alice smiled and nodded. "Yes, she is. She's also starving, but we'll have to feed her little bits at a time, or she'll get sick. I'll go and warm up some milk for her to begin with."

When she returned, the two older boys were still rubbing the dog gently with cloths, and John lay on his tummy, staring into her eyes. "She's not sad now," he lisped. "She just needs love."

Alice agreed silently and wondered what on earth she should do. The dog must have belonged to someone. She seemed gentle—and used to people. Although not professing to be a canine expert, to Alice she looked remarkably like a purebred Huntaway.

"I'll get on the phone right away in case someone is

looking for her." Alice's voice sounded hollow, even to her own ears, and she hesitated at the kitchen door, glancing back at the dog who was lapping messily at the warm milk. After licking up the last drop, she collapsed on the grass and closed her eyes.

Even after living in the district for a relatively short period, Alice understood that the best way of sharing something with other peninsula residents was by asking the telephone exchange. It was not exactly a congested depot, and the operators seemed to know more about the goings-on in the area than the local police did. Information could flow through the wires almost as quickly as by word of mouth.

She returned to the children with a trickle of optimism that boosted everyone's spirits. No one had lost or seen any stray dogs in the district and the operator seemed as puzzled as she was. The boys were draped over and around the sleeping hound and they looked up at their mother simultaneously, their faces filled with hope.

"Can we keep her?" George said.

"Please, Mum?" Timmy added.

John wrapped his arms around the dog's neck again and snuggled against her side.

Alice faltered, chewing her lip before she answered. "I suppose so."

CHAPTER 11

Innisfree
Kingseat
10 June 1938

Dear Alice,

Thank you for your letters—I received four this week and was so relieved to hear you're all well and to read your latest news.

We've been busy here, although I couldn't really say anything special has been happening. The children are back at school, and I managed to attend the Women's Division meeting last week. We catered for an auction sale held last Saturday, and my cream sponges were in demand, which gave me a boost. In spite of my love of cooking, I'm pleased it wasn't me having to feed all those men during shearing though—I commend you! It's enough for me to contribute to all the local gatherings.

Speaking of which, tomorrow the Hunt Club will be riding over our property as it's our district's turn to host the meet. Dougal has been out with his workers, trimming the hedges and ensuring the rails are sitting firmly on the wire fences they're to jump. I enjoy the spectacle of the adult's hunt so much more than the children's meet. It's quite an adrenalin rush seeing the beautifully turned-out horses and riders flow across the paddock and over the jumps after the hounds—and I'm glad we have no foxes in New Zealand, so it can all be more of an outing and not a blood sport! Dragging a scent for the hounds to follow seems so much more civilised. In spite of being proud of the children (especially looking so spick and span in their riding clothes and with the ponies plaited and shiny), I get very nervous seeing them all galloping madly across the paddocks. I suppose you miss all these social gatherings now.

James telephoned last week to advise that he has been nominated for our local council. No doubt he will do a good job should he be voted in.

I put some pansies on Emmie's grave last Sunday. It was pouring rain, so I was only able to say a quick prayer for her before taking refuge in the church. Father is failing fast, and I suspect he will not be here much longer.

I'm quite enjoying playing the piano at church now and am pleased you convinced me to do so. I'm not the pianist you are, but at least we no longer have to put up with poor Mrs Webster's painful attempts.

I look forward to hearing your latest news and send my love to you all,

Your loving sister,
Maud

Alice folded the letter and stoked the fire again. She looked through the window at the little boy lying in the sun next to the big black dog and flushed with love for them both. John was leaning against the dog's belly with a book held aloft as he 'read'. Unable to recognise much more than his own name, John could nevertheless recite his favourite fairy tale—*Jack and the Beanstalk*—and the dog didn't know the difference.

No longer the pitiful bag of bones that had followed the boys home, her dark coat had taken on a shine that matched her deep brown eyes and, although ribs still showed through her skin, her mournful appearance had brightened, and she walked with both her head and tail held high. Due to both Alice and Harry's failed attempts at locating any previous owner, the dog remained on Fantail Ridge, showing no interest in either leaving or helping Rock with stock work. She seemed to consider herself an essential service by simply hovering around the house yard and accompanying the boys wherever they went.

Alice looked at the clock and shot to her feet. It was almost noon, and she hadn't begun to prepare lunch for the men. Lifting the tea towel, she tapped the bread on the cooler beside the stove. Cringing at the sight of her fingernails, she turned her hands over to inspect them. Vince had called in with the mail while she was working in the vegetable garden and she had given them only a cursory wash in her haste to read Maud's letter. Plunging them into the bucket of cold water, she scrubbed the dirt from her palms and nails and dried them, inspecting them again. The cracks around the tips of her fingers had become more painful as the cold weather increased, and she reached for the pot of lanolin that sat on the windowsill. Rubbing a blob on her palm, she worked the cream into her dry, scaly digits while she decided what to prepare.

A few minutes later, she wrapped the slabs of bread filled with cold meat and homemade chutney in lettuce leaves and lay them on the tea towel in the bottom of the basket. She added enamel mugs, tea, and a jar of milk to the bucket holding the billy and lastly placed a tin filled with yesterday's madeira cake beside the sandwiches.

"Come on, John. We have to take lunch out to the men now."

The little boy closed the book and jumped to his feet, turning to the dog, and calling, "You can come too, Flossie."

Alice held John's hand as they walked across the lawn and down to the sheep yards, while Flossie trotted happily behind, slumping in a heap again when they reached the shed.

She rested the basket on the shelf below the row of bridles and other harness and reached up to gather the appropriate tack. Duke grazed nearby, and Alice called him as she fished out the piece of bread from her apron pocket. He nickered and strode purposefully towards her, nudging her gently as he pulled the crust from her hand. While he chewed, she dragged the sled out from under its shelter and put the collar over his neck. Then she slid the bit into his mouth, flicking the saliva off her hand before pulling the headpiece over his ears and beginning the process of threading the reins through the rings on the collar and belly band. She tightened the girth and backed the horse into the shafts. "Good boy. You're such a clever horse, aren't you?" She reassured him gently and patted his neck as she fastened the traces. "Hop up, John. You can be in charge of Duke while I get the basket."

John scrambled into the wooden contraption, beaming as he grasped the reins and waited while Alice slid the basket behind the bench seat and glanced across to Flossie.

"You can come, but you'll have to walk."

The dog jumped to her feet and wagged her tail, as though grateful to have been invited, even if it did mean she would have to exert a bit of energy.

Alice laughed and clicked the horse encouragingly.

The discovery of the old sled under the woolshed during their first winter on Fantail Ridge had been as exciting as a pot of gold. Without wheels, it slid quietly over both grass and mud, avoiding the risk of getting bogged, and for Alice, it offered the perfect alternative of walking and potentially having to carry a tired child. Once John was bigger, they might ride, but even that still posed the problem of transporting equipment, or even lunch, around the farm. With the continuing depressive state of the economy and increasing fuel prices, best of all, the sled cost nothing to operate, with the exception of grass and hay for the horse.

John held the reins while Alice opened and shut gates, and they made their way steadily towards the hills that swept in an east-west direction across the farm, their steep slopes coated with tea tree. A gap in the scrub was being carved out, angled in a steady scar from the flat land below the ridge to a dip at the top where one hill fell away and the next one began. Two figures grew larger as the sled drew near, their backs bent as they rhythmically hacked at the trunks of the sturdy shrubs.

"Cooee! Lunchtime."

The men both stopped immediately, swinging their axes over their shoulders as they turned towards the arrivals.

"You're a welcome sight. I'm starving." Harry wiped a sweaty face on his khaki shirt sleeve and reached for the billy of water on the ground. A dipper was tied to its handle, and Harry filled it and drank thirstily.

"Thank you, Mrs Alice." Paddy grinned and bent over the jacket lying in the shade. He removed his hat and dropped it on the jacket before hobbling the few yards to the stream and washing his hands and face.

The water tinkled over the stony-bottomed creek,

and John kicked off his gumboots and socks. "Can I paddle, Mum? It's not too cold."

Before she had a chance to answer, he was hurrying towards the stream with his four-legged friend close behind.

"That dog looks like she's got no intention of leaving," Paddy said.

"Hmm. Not sure whether I'm happy about that yet. We need another working dog, but this one doesn't look very interested," Harry added.

"I think she's been starved for so long she doesn't have her energy back. We need to give her time," Alice said.

Harry shook his head slowly and returned her grin. She knew perfectly well that he was becoming as attached to Flossie as she and the boys were. He just didn't want to admit it.

It had been Harry who had eventually named her. *"I think she should be Flossie. I remember having a dog very similar to her when I was young, and she was the best dog we ever had."*

Alice had suggested they call her Pilgrim, but John insisted she should be called Tip because of the white hairs on the end of her tail.

Harry looked at Alice and they grinned at each other. He might pretend to be still coming to terms with a dog hanging around the place, showing no interest or inclination in earning her keep, but Alice knew how soft-hearted he was. The dog was here to stay.

Alice unpacked the basket while Harry built a small fire with the dry tea tree twigs and set the billy to boil.

"How much longer will it take to clear a track?"

He studied the hill and rubbed his chin. "I reckon we'll have it clean enough to drag the harrows up here in another week or two. Then we'll move the cattle in and start feeding them hay on the track. That way they'll trample the debris down and by the end of winter we should be able to drive the truck up here."

Alice looked forward to the track's completion. Although she didn't get the opportunity to explore the farm very often, the day was getting closer when John would also be at school and she would have time to help with stock work, riding regularly over the farm. Gazing up the hill, she stood quietly, listening to the birds in the trees and the wind sigh above them.

"Why don't you go up and have a look?" Harry said. "We'll watch John and rest a while."

Alice needed no encouragement. She tied her headscarf more firmly under her chin and began climbing.

At the top western corner of their farthest paddock, a wide, fenced lane began, traversing the ridge and joining two other farms with a government-owned right-of-way. Alice had never been along the track but had heard that it led to the end of a gazetted road. In the future, there were plans to subdivide much of the rough country on either side of that road into numerous small farms, however, when that was likely to happen was anyone's guess. In the meantime, Harry had explored part of the track and described the incredible view across thousands of acres in every direction of the peninsula.

By the time she reached the top, Alice was puffing hard, and she undid the buttons on her jacket, allowing the cool breeze to waft across her chest. She was still half a mile or more from the boundary fence, but even from where she stood, the view was spectacular. To her left, bush-clad hills rolled down towards the Tasman ocean. Today the sea was dark grey, with huge waves rolling in, driven by strong westerly winds. Spindrift rose over the sand dunes, appearing as a light mist hovering above the land. She turned her back to the wind, gazing along the ridge to the Kaipara Harbour. It too was rough, with white-capped waves washing in to meet the mudflats of low tide. On the far side of the harbour, the mainland was just visible, its shadowy depths dark on the horizon.

The sun slid out from behind a cloud, and its gentle warmth on her back reminded Alice that the day was progressing quickly. She buttoned her jacket again and marched towards the top of the rough descent. A smile swept across her face as a hare zigzagged down the track in front of her. Touching her hands to her warm cheeks, she threw her arms wide and spun in a circle.

She was free, invigorated, and grateful to be alive.

CHAPTER 12

It was late that night when the phone rang—long, short, short, long. Alice sat bolt upright and listened as the ringing was repeated.

She leapt out of bed and grabbed the receiver from its hook as Harry struggled to his feet.

"Hello." A muffled voice echoed through the line and Alice frowned. "Maudie. Is that you?"

"Yes. I'm sorry it's so late but James rang to say Father has gone."

Alice reached for a chair as her face paled and she slumped silently into it. The clock ticked loudly, and she squinted at its hands, taking a few seconds to absorb the time. A quarter past ten.

"Say that again. It's hard to hear you, and I'm not fully awake yet."

Harry placed his hand on her shoulder, and she grasped it tightly in hers. She nodded into the receiver as Maud repeated her message, adding, *"The funeral is being arranged for Wednesday at eleven o'clock. Can you come?"*

"Yes, that will be fine. We'll be there." She paused and turned to face her husband. "Thanks, Maud. See you then. Good night."

"Good night. I'm looking forward to seeing you."

"Me too. Bye for now." Alice replaced the received and sighed.

"Father died earlier this evening. The funeral will be next Wednesday."

"Oh." Harry met her eyes, and they sat mutely for a few moments.

"What shall we do? I mean, the boys can't come and they're not old enough to be left at home?" Alice twisted her fingers together and held them to her mouth.

"What time is the funeral?"

"Maud said eleven o'clock. I suppose it suits everyone best, allowing family and friends time to get there and home again in the one day. That includes us?"

"I see. Yes, if we left here before dawn, we should arrive in plenty of time and be home again that night. I'm sure Paddy would help the boys get to school on time."

"What about John though? It's too much responsibility for Paddy to have to mind him all day when he'll have to do the chores as well?" A vision of Irene's kind face flashed in front of Alice. "Unless … do you think it would be too much for me to ask Irene to mind John for the day?"

Harry shrugged. "I'm sure with seven children of her own, another one will barely be noticed."

Alice sighed again and stood up. "We'll sleep on it and everything will be clear in the morning."

———

"It's too much for you. You have enough work with your own children," Alice protested.

Her reluctance in asking Irene to care for John had been unfounded, as the minute Alice mentioned her father's funeral, her friend jumped in and volunteered to mind all three boys. "Rubbish. The older ones will be at school anyway, and John can keep my little ones company for the day. Everyone will love it. I'll meet John at the school in the morning—he can walk with the older boys—and bring him home here. You let Paddy know that the children will come to me after school, and I'll give them tea before Jack runs them home at bedtime."

Alice thanked her profusely while Irene poured them both a second cup of tea.

Walking home at a brisk pace and leading Stormy, John clinging to his mane and chattering happily, Alice's mind filled with plans for the day away from the farm.

I'll bake a cake and pudding to leave with Irene and make a stew that will take care of Paddy's hunger and will provide a late-night meal for Harry and I. Paddy can supervise the boys' breakfast, and George and Timmy are both responsible enough to ensure John walks to school with them and is handed safely over to Irene.

While she unbridled the pony and released him to join his friends, a sudden surge of guilt brought her to a standstill. Since Maud's phone call the previous night, she had not shed one tear for her father.

———

As arranged, the following Wednesday morning, she and Harry left before dawn.

Wrapped warmly in her best coat and hat, Alice breathed a sigh of relief when they arrived with half an hour to spare. Maud and Dougal were standing on the roadside and Dougal leapt out and guided them to a space beside their own vehicle. After hugging each other tightly and both talking at once, Alice shifted her gaze from Maud to the crowd forming outside the church. Other family members were milling around, and she tucked her hand into the crook of Harry's elbow, met Maud's eyes and plastered a sympathetic smile on her face as they stepped onto the path and entered the cold stone building.

Flanked by their husbands, Alice and Maud clasped hands as they sang 'Abide with Me' and stared at the altar and oak casket that contained the body of their father. Behind them, the church was full, and when they turned to file outside, friends and relations that Alice had little or no recollection of nodded solemnly while she willed the expected tears to fill her eyes.

She knew the drill. In such a large family, there were always births, deaths, and marriages. This time, however, it was as though she was floating above the crowd, like a silent hawk on the wing, observing the gamut of emotions displayed by the attendees below, both real and forced. With the exception of the close relationship she held with Maud, Alice suddenly realised the family bonds had been, if not broken, at least stretched. At the age of thirty-eight, she was free of the obligations and constraints under which she had been raised. She was her own person—a strong, loving wife and mother—and the promises she and Harry had made to one another could now blossom.

"Are you hungry?" Maud whispered in her ear.

"Starving," Alice replied.

Linking elbows and followed by their husbands, now deep in conversation, they headed for the church hall.

The usual spread set out on trestle tables was rapidly consumed, and it was after two o'clock before Alice and Harry, Maud, and Dougal slipped away to stand at Emmie's little grave. Mid-winter provided few flowers, but Maud had managed to snip a neat posy of hellebores and cyclamen from her garden to lay against the headstone.

Softly, the sisters sang the first verse of 'All Things Bright and Beautiful' before turning back to the crowd to say their farewells.

When they stepped through the shed door late that evening, Alice and Harry were welcomed by three drowsy boys sitting around the table listening to a story recited by Paddy.

Alice smiled, her weary body bursting with love as she hugged each of them in turn. They were home.

CHAPTER 13

Two weeks later, heavy clouds clung to the hills, and Alice had to put a match to the kerosene lamp in the middle of the day as the light struggled through the two small windows.

Leaving immediately after breakfast, Harry and Paddy were anxious to complete the scrub cutting before the weather deteriorated. Progress had been hampered by the steep, uneven ridges, and the last thing they needed was heavy rain triggering a landslide.

In the corner of their bedroom, Alice sat at the Singer sewing machine, treading furiously on the rocking foot peddle in order to finish the pile of mending that overflowed the basket beside her. After each knee patch or trouser hem, she got up and peered out the window to check on her charges. Gratitude for the big dog brought a smile to her face.

Her devotion to John had removed a large portion of Alice's supervisory responsibilities as the dog whined or scratched at the door if John strayed from his dedicated play area—a patch of sandy dirt immediately outside the door that the child had claimed as his.

She reached for the next pair of trousers, frowning as she recalled the comment Harry had made at breakfast. *"Ed had the strangest look on his face when he saw our shearing plant. It was almost as though he suddenly remembered something but then forgot again."*

"Did you say anything?" Alice had asked.

"No. He's so private I feel uncomfortable questioning him —and he offers so little. I didn't think it was important, just a bit odd?"

While she puzzled over the strange, silent man from the wharf, she peeped through the window again. Her face softened at the vision of John pushing a hand-me-down toy truck around in the dirt. Flossie lay next to him, alternating between loud snores and occasional sighs as she opened an eye and changed position.

With the exception of John and Flossie, the yard was silent. The builders had headed to Auckland for a family wedding and seemed unable to nominate when they would return. At the thought, her blood pumped with frustration. The new house was almost finished, and she was dying to move in. However, the painters couldn't come until the weather improved, and the plumber was still waiting for one of the new septic tanks to arrive. Alice sighed in defeat. There was no other option but show patience.

She leapt, pricking her finger on the machine needle when Flossie began to bark. Deep, deafening booms emitting from the dogs throat galvanised her into a run from the kitchen, leaving the door wide open behind her. The dog had got to her feet and was galloping across the grass towards the front gate with John chasing after her. They both stopped at the fence and Alice caught up, pausing as alarm flooded her veins. Her chest tightened at the sight of Paddy approaching, his bandy, deformed legs shuffling in a wild, uncontrolled manner.

"Mrs Alice. Mrs Alice. It's Harry!" Paddy could barely breathe as he gasped out the words. His hat was gone, and his hair stood straight up from his head in uneven spikes. His shirt tail flapped loosely over his trousers.

"What's happened?"

"Cut his leg. Real bad. Blood everywhere. With the axe."

"Oh my goodness. Where is he? On the hill?"

"At the bottom where we eat lunch. Come quickly."

A cold shiver ran down her spine as dread crept through her. For a moment, her legs refused to move, weighted down with fear. Then, as adrenaline kicked in, her head cleared and she registered Paddy's pale, frightened face. "Go and catch Duke and get him harnessed to the sled. I'll get the first aid kit and see if I can raise anyone on the telephone. John, go with Paddy and help him."

She didn't wait to see the old man and little boy hurry away but turned and sprinted back to the shed.

"Please, please answer," she whispered. She held the receiver to her ear and furiously wound the handle on the side of the wooden box.

"Exchange, which number do you want?" The voice was calm and efficient, and Alice raised her face, closing her eyes briefly in thanks.

"It's Alice Simpson here. There's been an accident. I need help please. My husband has cut his leg."

"Don't worry, Mrs Simpson. I'll telephone your neighbours and see what help I can get. Where exactly is he?"

"Right at the back of the farm. I'm going there now to see what I can do and will try to get him home." Her voice rose in panic and she stopped.

"You go to him now, Mrs Simpson, and leave the rest to me."

Alice dropped the receiver back on the hook and reached for the tin of first aid items from the shelf beside the tea caddy. Hurriedly opening the linen chest, she hauled out a couple of towels and a worn sheet that was now equal parts patches and original cotton fabric. Then, grabbing the hand-washing bucket, she threw the water over the lemon tree outside before stuffing the collection of items into the vessel. She tied her scarf over her head, collected both hers and John's coats, and slammed the door behind her.

The bucket bumped against her legs as she ran across the horse paddock towards the shed. Clutching the sled for a moment, she regained her breath. Duke was already partially harnessed, and he stamped a hoof as though comprehending the urgency of the situation and anxious to be on his way. Alice placed the gear onto the sled and hastily buckled the final straps on his harness. Then she swiped up the horse's canvas rug, threw it on the wooden tray, and stepped aboard. "Get up, Duke. As fast as you can."

John clung to his mother as the sled jolted across the grass. Paddy slumped on the hard wooden seat, his face ghostly and his eyes wide. Duke had never travelled over the farm any faster than a brisk walk, but as soon as they moved through the gateway and faced the open paddock, he swung into his long, racing stride, and they covered the distance at a frightening speed, slowing only to cross gullies and open and shut gates.

In spite of their rapid transit, the journey seemed interminable, and Alice's pulse thumped deafeningly in her ears. Flossie overtook the sled and bounded ahead of them, carving a path through the startled sheep. She made no sound until she reached Harry's side and sniffed him. Then she turned towards Alice and let out a long, terrifying howl.

Alice fell on her knees and hugged Harry, hiding her shock at his pale, clammy face. He struggled to raise himself to his elbows, and she gently pushed him back down again.

"Don't move, love. We're here now."

She turned her gaze to his legs and glanced up at Paddy.

"I tied my belt around to slow the bleeding," he whispered.

Alice nodded. She was not a nurse and had never witnessed a serious accident, but deep in the recesses of her memory, she recalled being told that bleeding can be slowed with a tourniquet. In this case, the belt seemed to have done the trick, and the blood pooling on the limb had congealed to a sticky, black mess. She ripped Harry's trouser leg open and inspected the wound.

Flinching, she swallowed the bile that rose in her throat and studied the deep cut in Harry's shin. Just to the right of the bone, a deep, angry gash ran on an angle, penetrating flesh, muscle, and numerous blood vessels. She glanced over to John, thankful that he seemed more concerned with Flossie than his father.

"Fetch some clean water please, Paddy? John, you look after Flossie and make sure she doesn't run away." The possibility of that occurring was zero, but Alice hoped it would at least keep his attention off his injured father.

While the old man hobbled to the stream, Alice began to tear the sheet into strips of varying widths. Then, avoiding the wound itself, she gently wiped clumps of dried blood off Harry's leg, removing leaves and bits of tea tree bark that clung to his skin.

"How did it happen?" Alice watched her husband's face, now almost blue beneath its lingering tan. Sweat beaded on his forehead, and his voice was strained and weak, elevating Alice's anxiety to a new height.

"I don't really remember. My foot slipped and I went down, but I'm not sure whether the axe hit my leg before or after my fall?"

"Shh. Rest now." She stroked his face gently and kissed his forehead, reassuring him as best she could. Then she turned to his injury.

After folding a clean pad of cotton fabric, she placed it over the wound and began bandaging his leg from the ankle to above the knee. With Paddy's help, they backed Duke as close to Harry as possible, edging the sled under his shoulders, then, tucking the towels underneath him, they hauled him gently, inch by inch, until he lay on the timber platform. Alice quickly gathered up their belongings and indicated to Paddy to take hold of Duke's bridle. The poor man was shaking, his energy spent, and he seemed unable to think for himself.

Alice covered Harry with the horse rug and sat John next to Paddy on the tiny bench seat. Then, walking beside the horse and with Flossie following solemnly behind, the procession began its painful journey over the farm towards the house.

They were halfway across the valley when the

clouds opened up and rain drummed down, saturating the sorry little group within seconds. Alice turned the canvas rug around, rigging a cover that, held at the front by Paddy, stretched over his head and back and included Harry and John. Her thick, woollen skirt bumped against her legs as it absorbed the rain, and her feet squelched in her gumboots. She brushed the water from her eyes, ignoring the hair that stuck in wet rat-tails to her face.

They were almost back to the woolshed, the rain still sheeting down and reducing visibility to almost nothing, when a truck slithered down the paddock in the mud. The doors were flung open, and Vince and Clive jumped out, while another two leapt from the back tray.

Without wasting precious time, they scooped Harry off the sled and transferred him to a pile of woolpacks that lay in the back of the truck. The rain continued to run off their hats and soak their clothes as they made Harry as comfortable as possible. Clive and one of the other men covered him with a tarpaulin and settled down on each side of him as Vince slid into the driver's seat.

"We'll take him straight to the hospital, and I'll ring you from there," Vince shouted above the rain.

"I can follow you in the car."

"No. It's too wet, and we can't have you getting bogged on the road. Stay here with your family—at least until the rain stops." His voice held a commanding tone that Alice had never heard before, and she froze for a second. She let his comments sink in and nodded as her mind flicked to her sons. They would be home from school soon—wet and cold—and would need her.

She raised her hand in farewell as the truck drove away and only then allowed the tears to slide down her cheeks.

"What shall we do, Mrs Alice?"

Paddy's voice penetrated her consciousness, and she brushed the tears away before turning. She reached out and lay her hand on his arm.

"We'll unharness Duke then go inside. I'll get you some dry clothes and make a cup of tea."

Raiding the airing cupboard, Alice dragged out a pair of Harry's trousers, socks, and an old hand-knitted jersey. She handed them to Paddy and draped a towel over his shoulder. "Get out of those wet things, Paddy. I'm sorry the water's not hot enough for us all to have a bath, but a wash and dry clothes will help." She turned to John and held out her hand. "Come on, love. Let's get you cleaned up too."

She stoked the fire and stirred the rice pudding that had been sitting in the oven since mid-morning. Harry's favourite. A lump caught in her throat, and as Paddy and John devoured a piece of cake each, she swallowed her tea and prayed for her husband as she had not prayed since before whooping cough took her little Emmie.

CHAPTER 14

For once Alice was glad that her afternoon was too busy to dwell on what might be. George and Timmy arrived home like a pair of drowned rats, happy to soak in a hot bath while Alice explained their father's plight as best she could. In silence, everyone wrapped their hands around a mug of cocoa and shared anxious glances. The kitchen had never been so quiet. Even the clock's ticking seemed to slow. While she hovered, she glanced repeatedly at the phone, prepared dinner, folded, then ironed the previous day's washing and encouraged the boys to sit at the table and complete a jigsaw puzzle. The phone remained silent as Paddy donned an oilskin coat, sou'wester hat, and dry boots.

"I'll feed the animals." A gust of cold, damp air whooshed through the open door, and he slammed it quickly behind him.

Darkness had fallen by the time he returned, clutching a large handful of beans.

"Looks like this is the last of them, Mrs Alice."

"Thank you, Paddy. Yes, I'm surprised you found any. I've been meaning to pull the vine out and dig some sheep manure into the bed."

Alice gathered cutlery from the drawer and began to set the table. Her insides were coiled in a knot, and eating was the last thing on her mind. Still, she had a duty to care for her family, and so she served herself the smallest meal she could in order to avoid Paddy's questioning gaze. The boys' appetites seemed undeterred, and even Paddy ate everything she dished up. It was when she spooned the rice pudding into bowls that her throat constricted, her stomach heaved, and she dashed outside.

Minutes later, she wiped her mouth and slipped past the window into the wash house. She sluiced her face under the cold tap and drew a deep breath. *Harry could be in hospital for a while. I need to pull myself together. What would he do if it was me?*

She snatched the towel from the rail and patted her cheeks dry. Then she straightened her shoulders and returned to her family. The boys looked up, hesitated briefly, and returned to scraping their bowls clean. Only Paddy fixed his gaze on her. Alice gave him a glimmer of a smile as she caught the telltale mist in his eyes.

It was late when she poured another cup of tea for

herself and Paddy and slumped back into the chair. The boys had finally drifted off to sleep, but the man across the table, sipping silently at his drink, showed no sign of retiring to his quarters.

"You look so tired, Paddy. Are you sure you don't want to go to bed?"

"No, Mrs Alice. I couldn't sleep if I tried." He dropped his gaze into his cup, and Alice started as the cup rattled in the saucer. "It should have been me."

"What should have been you, Paddy?"

"The accident."

Alice's exhaustion faded, and she leaned forward and reached for his hand. "Don't think like that. It was no one's fault." She paused, frowning. "Why would you think it should have been you?"

"Because I've always been a no good."

Alice opened her mouth to reply, closing it again as he shook his head.

"I want to tell you. I've been wanting to tell you for a long time."

"I'm listening." Alice pushed her cup and saucer aside and clasped her hands together, her elbows resting on the table.

"I was a foundling. One of those babies who was dumped in a workhouse in Dublin. I don't know who my parents were or why I was put there, but I was."

"Go on," she whispered.

"Somehow I survived. I don't know how, because there was never much food and those around me died like flies in the filth. Mostly from starvation and disease. But when I was a few years old, maybe eight or nine, I was sent to work for a man called O'Donohue. He had racehorses, a hard man. Treated the horses better than his staff. I was lucky that the stable manager—a bloke called Finn—was kind. He protected me from the worst of O'Donohue's temper. In return for his protection, I went to Dublin with Finn and got caught up in the 1916 Irish Rebellion. They called it the Easter Rebellion. Anyway, things went bad, and I ran away and stowed on a boat to England. I did what I could to stay alive until the end of the war—you don't need to know what. Then I got a job on a New Zealand ship that was bringing troops home. I jumped ship here and drifted from job to job, getting whatever I could. My bad legs held me back a bit, but I eventually got work on a farm near New Plymouth, with an elderly couple who didn't have the money to pay me but instead fed me quite well and taught me how to read."

Alice wriggled in her chair as silence fell in the room. "Go on," she urged.

"I had taken the wagon into town to collect supplies for them, and there was a terrible storm. A landslide behind their house killed them both before I got back home, so I moved on. Came north, and that's when I got the job with Harry's family."

An ache filled Alice's soul, and she reached her hand across the table and squeezed Paddy's.

"So you see. I should have been the one who was injured. I don't deserve to be here."

Alice jumped to her feet and leaned forward. "Paddy. You do deserve to be here. More than anyone. Look at your life. You haven't exactly been short of opportunities to die, but you didn't. In my book, that means you are meant to be here, with us, and there's no more to be said about it." She kept her voice low, with a steel edge to it that even she barely recognised.

The wind howled around the shed and rain slashed at the windows while the two of them stared at each other. Paddy drew in a deep, shuddering breath and hung his head.

Alice quietly moved around the table and lay her arm over his shoulders. She cleared her throat and blinked rapidly. "You are part of our family now, Paddy, and we appreciate you. Your past is your business, and I only wish it had been more pleasant for you. But it doesn't matter to us, and you must believe me when I say that this is your home."

Before he could answer, the phone rang—its shrill bell startling them both.

Alice dived for the receiver and gripped it tightly.

"Is that Mrs Simpson?"

"Yes, this is she. Alice Simpson."

"Matron here. I want to let you know that Doctor has cleaned and sutured the wound, and your husband will need to stay in hospital until healing is progressing and the stitches can come out."

Alice released the breath she didn't realise she had been holding until then.

"Can we come and see him?" she asked tentatively.

"Give him forty-eight hours to recover and then you may visit between two and four in the afternoon."

"Thank you Matron." She hesitated for a moment. "Can I bring the children?"

"I'm sorry Mrs Simpson. Children are not allowed."

"Oh, I see. Well then, I shall be in the day after tomorrow."

"Thank you. That will be appreciated. Goodnight Mrs Simpson."

"Goodnight."

She hung up the receiver and turned to meet Paddy's long, anxious face. "As you no doubt gathered, that was Matron. I am allowed to visit him in two days but children are not welcome."

Paddy sighed and pushed himself to his feet. "Well, that's something I suppose."

They stared at each other for a minute before he spoke again.

"Regardless of hospital rules restricting children, for me they are always welcome, no matter the circumstances—your three boys mean the world to me." He gave a small nod and moved towards the door. "I'd better try to get some sleep then. We've got plenty to keep us busy."

Alice's chin quivered as he shrugged into the oilskin coat and pulled his hat over his ears.

"Goodnight, Mrs Alice. And … thank you."

———

SHE STOOD STARING AT THE CLOSED DOOR FOR A FULL five minutes after Paddy left. Then she climbed the ladder and studied her sleeping boys. Her face softened. Love for her children filled her chest and tangled with the web of compassion for Paddy.

It was only in the hour before dawn that she finally drifted off to sleep, tossing and turning as visions of Harry's white face and a river of blood plagued her.

The watery sunlight filtered through the bedroom window, and she gave up trying to get back to sleep. She lay staring at the sheet of plywood that served as a ceiling, exhausted, totally drained of all thoughts. After throwing back the eiderdown, she crossed to the window and peered out. The rain had stopped, and a misty freshness lay over the land.

Her breath fogged up the glass, and she shivered. After dressing quickly, she snapped a handful of dry twigs, prodding the fire into life. While the kettle slowly came to the boil, she set the pan on the hob, sliced bacon and dropped it into the hot fat, stepping back as it sizzled and spat. Her stomach growled. Harry's pig-hunting expedition with Vince and Clive in early autumn had provided them all with fresh pork, and Vince's attempt at curing the bacon had been welcomed by them all. It made a nice change from mutton and fish—and the option of enjoying bacon and eggs for breakfast instead of porridge was a treat.

Whether it was the smell of bacon frying or because of the events of the previous day, Paddy and the boys joined Alice in the kitchen earlier than usual.

As soon as they had finished eating, she shared her thoughts. "We don't know how long Dad will be in hospital, and when he does come home, he won't be able to do his usual work."

Four pairs of eyes stared at her, their depths a kaleidoscope of colour and questions.

"Paddy, I'd be grateful if you would continue taking care of the stock. Of course, the boys and I will help as much as possible, especially feeding out hay. Would you mind also continuing to milk Josie? George and Timmy, I need you both to be as grown up as possible. The wood box needs to be kept full and …" She trailed off as George opened his mouth and then closed it again. "George?"

"The rams. They've been with the ewes since shearing, so we'll have to get them out soon."

Alice looked at Paddy. "How urgent is that?"

"They'll be right for another couple of weeks."

"Good. I'll phone Irene and see if she would look after John for me when I go into town, and I'll also find out what the road condition is like."

"What about us, Mum?" Timmy asked.

"I'll be here when you get home from school each day, and we'll all continue as we usually do. If I can get into town to visit Dad, I'll be home again before dark, so you needn't worry."

"Never fear, Mum. I'll look after Timmy, and we can peel the potatoes and do stuff like that."

Alice beamed at George and collected the dirty plates from the table. "Wonderful. Well, we might as well make a start now. I'll fill the sink, and you boys can wash and dry the dishes before you get ready for school while I make your lunches. Then I have lots of dirty washing to catch up on."

"OH MY GOODNESS. DO WE REALLY OWN THAT MANY clothes?"

"Me and Flossie will feed the chooks." John darted outside, and Alice rested her hands on her hips as she studied the piles of dirty laundry on the wash house floor.

While the fire built up and the water in the copper began to heat, she added soap flakes and sorted the washing, dropping the cleanest of the heaps into the water. Working methodically through the piles from cleanest to dirtiest, she eventually hung the final load on the line in time to prepare lunch.

Her mind was a tangle as her concern for Harry, farm and household chores, and the return of the builders all vied for attention in her head. She wanted to discuss things with her husband as questions surfaced that she had no answer for. Paddy was a wonderful worker, but she accepted that he was no leader. The past twenty-four hours had taken a toll on the old man, and she was almost as worried about him as she was Harry. The last thing he needed was to have her put pressure on him.

Shall I send a telegram to the builders and find out when they plan to return? How urgent is it to muster the sheep and draft off the rams? How long have the cattle been in that paddock and when should they be moved?

She stirred the soup and set the table for three. Yesterday's bread was almost gone, but if she sliced it a little more thinly than usual, there would be enough.

The hours following lunch were filled with mixing and kneading enough dough for two days, making pastry while the stew bubbled on the stove, and tidying away the sewing that she had abandoned the previous day.

Exhausted, she picked up her pen and writing pad from the sideboard, looked at the clock, and collapsed into a chair. She had half an hour before the boys would be home, so her letter would be short.

Fantail Ridge
South Head
22 June 1938

Dear Maud,
I hardly know where to begin. These past hours have

been a bit of a nightmare, but I suppose it could have been worse.

Harry had a scrub-cutting accident yesterday and is now in Helensville hospital. Somehow, he slipped, or the axe slipped (or both?) and he has a nasty gash on his leg. They have stitched him up and are keeping him confined to bed until it has healed enough for him to come home. Poor Paddy was a nervous wreck and is still not himself as he witnessed the whole thing. He's so fond of Harry. It must have given him an awful fright (as it did me when I saw it). He and I sat up late last night—until we received the call from the hospital. Poor man—he told me all about his childhood, and I struggled not to cry. Sometimes we think we had a tough childhood, but it was nothing to what he has endured in his life.

I'm not allowed to visit Harry until tomorrow and am waiting for advice about the road condition as we've had heavy rain. With the current king tides, sections of the low-lying areas will have been inundated, and I don't fancy sitting in axel-deep mud on my own—or actually at all for that matter! I am still a bit nervous driving the new Chevrolet. It is so much bigger and heavier than the Ford was, but I suppose the advantage is that it handles our road better (even if I don't!).

Irene will mind John for me as the new teacher has settled in well and she now has more time to herself (if that's a possibility with her big family?).

How did you get on with the Hunt Club riding over your land? I imagine it would have been a great spectacle and

Dougal would have loved it. Because of the rain, we haven't had any mail deliveries or even seen a vehicle drive past for days.

I'll send the boys down to Ed's with this letter as soon as they have eaten afternoon tea as the 'Wairua' is passing tonight and will collect mail (just in case it's too wet for me to get to town tomorrow). It's a shame the two passenger boats go past during the night, but I suppose they schedule the trips to meet the train for Auckland. Ed must either not need much sleep or is comfortable working strange hours as he seems hard to locate most of the time?

I am making a meat and vegetable pie, large enough for tea tonight and tomorrow. So if I'm late home, there's food that will just need heating. I can't bring myself to make rice pudding without Harry here. He loves it so much, and it makes me teary when I think of it, and I certainly won't cry in front of the children. Instead, I have a pudding in the steamer on the stove top, using the last of the golden syrup. I'm hoping to stock up again on grocery items tomorrow.

The boys are home now, so I'll sign off and get this on its way!

Love and blessings to you all,

Alice

Alice raised her face to soak up the freshness in the air. She took slow, deep breaths while the boys climbed into the car, slamming the doors behind them. Her hands clamped the steering wheel firmly and she reversed out of the shed, letting the air out of her lungs in a whoosh when she braked. She rubbed the clumsiness from her legs, plunged the clutch to the floor, and wrestled with the gear lever. The vehicle lumbered away slowly, giving a hop as she pressed her foot on the accelerator.

In the rear-view mirror, Paddy's solitary figure was shadowed by the large morose dog collapsed at his feet, its limbs crumpling in a disjointed heap. The children's flapping arms distracted Alice as they leaned out the windows, laughing and calling out their goodbyes in response to the old man's half-hearted wave. Flossie's gaze seemed to burn into her and Rock sat in front of the shed, his ears pricked and his head held in a regal pose.

Changing gear, Alice focused on the road, negotiating the steep turns before reaching the flat. The vision of Paddy remained in her head, and she bit her lip. He had seemed more purposeful this morning, even if seemingly unable to smile. *At least he will shift the cattle and attend to the daily chores—while he counts every minute until we return home.*

She halted outside the school, and George and Timmy jumped out of the car and ran towards the small group of children kicking a ball around on the grass.

"Your turn next, John."

The little boy sat on the bench seat beside her, his face alight with excitement. Although they tried to socialise every couple of weeks, farm work dictated their availability and gatherings were mostly short.

Once again, the farm truck blocked the entrance to the Bennett farm, and Alice turned off the engine and stepped carefully onto the driest patch of grass she could reach. She had dressed in her second-best skirt with a white blouse and warm, tailored jacket. About to slip her feet into her good shoes, she had hesitated and instead wrapped them in a piece of newspaper and slid her stockinged feet into gumboots. A telephone call from Ainsworth's early that morning had confirmed that, although muddy, the road was dry enough to get to town.

She had tucked her good shoes under the passenger's seat and lay newspaper on the floor. Smiling, she and John negotiated the muddy entrance to Bennett's farm. Her decision to wear boots had been the right one.

A barrage of children welcomed John at the door, and he gave Alice a quick wave as he ran after Hugh towards the swing.

"Come in." Irene welcomed Alice, and for a few seconds, she dithered while Irene waved to the older children. "Bye. Have a good day at school." Then she turned back to Alice and smiled. "Have you got time for a cup of tea?" Irene's tall, graceful figure and serene smile were like a soothing balm, and Alice's tummy rumbled.

"Thank you, I will." She slipped off her boots and entered the kitchen in her stockinged feet. She glanced at the Bennett's clock. A quarter to nine. Another half hour wouldn't matter. In fact, it would give the road a little more time to dry out, and the incoming tide was still hours away.

At nine-thirty, Alice gave Irene a hug and thanked her for the third time. The older woman's tranquillity and capable attitude had been exactly what she needed. Holding her head high, her anxieties eased. Of course the cup of tea and two hot scones with butter and honey helped, and her stomach had stopped its gymnastics—for the moment anyway.

The journey into town was slow and laborious as

the heavy Chevrolet slipped and slithered in the mud. Alice wrestled with the steering wheel, grateful she had the road to herself. At twenty miles per hour, she chugged along the flats, dropping to below ten on hills and around sharp bends. As the pale strip of gravel appeared in the distance, contrasting with the brown sludge on which she had just driven, Alice breathed a sigh of relief. She approached the smoother sections of road a few miles from town and stopped to change into her shoes, wrapping the dirty boots and stowing them in the rear of the vehicle.

The town clock chimed eleven-thirty as she climbed out of the car in the main street. A visit to the grocers, the drapery, and the post office for more stamps took Alice almost two hours as it seemed word of Harry's accident had arrived before she did. Those she met either wanted to stop and talk or passed by with a knowing look, as if dying to ask but afraid to intrude. It was a small community, and though her visits to town were infrequent, she welcomed the friendly attitude and sense of belonging. Harry was better known than she, and by all accounts, well respected if the invitations to join the local Federated Farmers Group and sporting clubs were anything to go by. Harry had thanked them kindly and advised that he would join just as soon as he could.

Alice entered the Why Not tea room, ordered a cup of tea and a sandwich, and collapsed into a chair. Anticipation and an anxious excitement filled her as she sipped her drink and counted the minutes until hospital visiting hours. In her bag, letters from George and Timmy and John's drawing of he and Flossie sat in a large, white envelope. They would bring a smile to Harry's face.

———

THE STENCH OF DISINFECTANT BURNED THE BACK OF HER throat, and her nostrils flared. *At least it should be free of bugs.* She trailed down the corridor, past the Matron's office and sluice room, pausing under the sign *Men's Ward*. The wail of a child echoed down the hall, followed by soft murmurings. She stood in the doorway and searched the area.

Three sterile-looking iron beds stood against either side of the room, six in all, their heads jammed against the wall and the foot-ends allowing a wide corridor down the centre. A large window directly opposite her let a flood of sunlight splash on the polished floor. Four beds stood empty, their bleached cotton sheets stiff and immaculate, while the one nearest to her was occupied by an elderly Maori man, his hair a fluffy white cloud against a deep brown face. His eyes were closed and his body so still that for a moment, Alice wasn't sure if he was alive or dead. She swung her gaze to the bed opposite and warmth surged through her.

She strode towards the bed and bent over her

husband, stroking his face as she kissed him gently. "Harry. It's me."

He opened his eyes and gave her a small grin. "Hello, me. It's good to see you."

"How are you feeling?"

"Not too bad." He grimaced as he attempted to sit up, and Alice put her arm under his, startled as his body heat burned into hers. She shoved a second pillow behind his back, alarm growing at his lack of strength.

Before she could comment, a nurse entered the room. "Mrs Simpson?"

"Yes, hello. I'm Alice, Harry's wife."

The nurse nodded then picked up Harry's wrist, frowning as she studied the watch hanging from her chest. After a minute, she patted his hand and directed a concerned gaze at Alice. "I'm going to get the doctor." Then she turned and swept briskly out of the room.

Alice gritted her teeth in an attempt to prevent herself from shaking as Harry closed his eyes. This was not what she had expected, and she looked around feverishly, wondering if there was something she should be doing.

"I'll be alright, love. Feeling a bit crook at the moment, but it'll take more than a cut on the leg to knock me down." Harry spoke so softly she had to lean forward to hear him.

Hurried, squeaky footsteps heralded the nurse with a tall, thin man in a white coat at her side. *The doctor?*

Matron sailed in behind him, rather like an ocean liner about to dock. Her stiff white veil hid any sign of hair, accentuating her round, chubby face.

With a commanding air, she laid her hand on Alice's arm. "Come with me, Mrs Simpson. Doctor will examine your husband and inform you of his findings shortly. Let me get you a cup of tea."

Alice's head spun. Judging by Matron's demeanour, she half-expected to be told off, for what she wasn't sure. However, the strength and efficient tone of the woman's voice suggested a kind streak flowed through her veins, and Alice allowed herself to be led into a waiting room, feeling rather like a lost dog.

It was empty, and Matron guided her to a hard, leather armchair. "Wait there. I'll be back in a moment."

And she was—carrying a small tray with two cups of tea on it. Following close behind was the doctor.

As they sipped their drinks, he questioned Alice about Harry's accident.

"I'm sorry. I really can't help you as I wasn't there and didn't see what happened. I only know it took us quite a while to get to him and then load him on the truck and … it rained, and we were all soaked to the skin. I suppose it would have been about three hours after the accident before the men delivered him here?"

She looked into the man's eyes and felt the blood drain from her face.

"Will he be alright?"

"We believe so. It's the infection that's the problem.

I've given him what they call an antibiotic. There are a couple of different drugs we have available to us now, but not all are effective for each and every need. So it may take some time before we get an improvement."

"So, what should I do?" Alice was so shocked her voice was barely a whisper.

"I suggest you go home, and we'll telephone when he is feeling a bit better and able to have you visit again."

"Oh." Alice stared at the man for a minute. She reached into her purse and pulled out the envelope. "Our sons wrote him letters. Would you give them to him please?"

The doctor smiled. A kind, gentle smile that softened his thin features and sent a glimmer of hope through Alice.

"Would you like to give them to him yourself? He's very sleepy, so I suggest you don't stay longer than a couple of minutes."

She nodded silently, and the doctor indicated for her to follow Matron again.

"Thank you," Alice said. Then she trailed the broad, white-uniformed woman back to Harry.

This time, she was prepared. She leaned over his bed and read the boys' letters to him. He blinked and gave her a brief smile as she held up John's drawing. Then, as drowsiness consumed him again, she stroked his forehead and placed the folded letters in his hand. "I'll be back to see you as soon as they let me."

"Alice." She bent her head close to his face as he whispered, "You're the best thing that's ever happened to me."

She squeezed his fingers and brushed the stray tear from her cheek. "And you're the best man in the world." She stood and swallowed, returning his wan smile. "So you hurry up and get better, because we can't live without you."

Squaring her shoulders, Alice edged quietly out of the room and marched up the road, not pausing until she reached the car. She checked the town clock. Ten minutes to three. Forcing the hospital visit to the back of her mind, she focused on her journey home and started the car. *The tide will be coming in again soon.* Alice pulled into the vacant area behind the grocers shop and switched off the engine. Before she had time to get out of the vehicle, a skinny teenaged boy emerged carrying a box twice as wide as himself. Alice hurried to the rear of the car and opened the boot, standing back as the lad stowed her order, then she thanked him and started for home.

Water was lapping the edge of the road by the time she passed the school. She drove on, content in the knowledge that Irene would be true to her word, meeting George and Timmy at three o'clock so John could walk home with his brothers. She hesitated as she crossed the heavy timber girders over the inlet, then stopped the car in the middle of road, got out, and walked back. Glancing across the creek, she barely registered the tips of mangroves poking above the water. Waves sloshed against the foot of the bridge, spraying droplets over her shoes. There was not a soul in sight.

Leaning on the railing, she stared into the water and let her tears flow. *I didn't even get to tell Harry about Paddy.* A seagull swooped above, calling in a high, raucous tone—as though questioning her presence, or perhaps her sobs.

She didn't know how long she stood there. A gust of cold wind buffeted her, and she shivered. Pulling a handkerchief from her pocket, she then mopped her face and returned to the car. The engine throbbed into life, and she accelerated up the hill.

My family will be waiting.

CHAPTER 16

For a moment, the red truck parked in the yard startled Alice—until she read the sign on the driver's door. A trickle of hope warmed her. *G.H. Batty, Plumber.*

She nosed the car into the shed and hurried through the gate into the house yard. Paddy and the boys were milling around what appeared to be a very large hole in the back yard while Flossie ran around its perimeter, barking and generally making a nuisance of herself.

"Mum!" John bolted towards her and threw his arms around her legs. "The man's here to do the s-spectic."

"The septic, sweetheart. For the toilet." She smiled as two heads popped up from the depths of the pit. The first appeared to belong to a man of around middle age and the other may have been his son. Both wore striped woollen hats that sat just above their eyebrows and beneath, their cheeks glowed plump and pink. The only difference seemed to be the thick folds of skin around the older man's neck and the bags under his eyes. Underneath it's coating of mud, the other appeared to have a bright, clear complexion.

"Hello there. I'm Alice Simpson."

"Pleasure, ma'am. Won't shake your hand. Bit dirty."

Something about the way the older man spoke made Alice want to reply in the same way—as though words were precious, and none should be wasted. "Been here long?"

The man heaved himself onto the grass, the younger lad following immediately behind. *A bit dirty is an understatement.* He was filthy. As they crawled out of the hole, Alice grimaced.

"I'm sorry. I would have been here if I had known," she added.

"Few hours. No one around, so got started."

"I see. I presume you have spoken to the builders?"

This time he gave a silent nod.

"So … did they give you any indication of when they would be returning?" Annoyance filtered into Alice's voice and she clamped her lips together and glanced at Paddy.

He clutched his hat, turning it around in his hands in a nervous twitch. "Tomorrow."

She raised her eyebrows and forced a smile. "Wonderful." She paused. *What would Harry say if he were here.*

She chided herself. *He would welcome them and ask them to join the family for meals.*

"H-how long will you be here? Would you like to wash up? Join us for tea?"

"Thank you. Got our beds. Good to clean up though. Meal would be nice." He nodded again. "Grant." Then he indicated with his thumb, and Alice looked at the lad. "Jack."

"Pleased to meet you, Grant and Jack. Now, if you would like to clean up in the wash house, we'll see you shortly for your meal."

———

IN THE KITCHEN, EVERYONE SEEMED TO TALK AT ONCE. The boys were enthusiastically relaying their after-school activities to their mother, as though vying for importance in their father's absence. John pointed to the pile of wood he had brought in, and Timmy assured her that the dogs and chooks had been fed.

"I helped Paddy feed the cattle, and we used Duke to pull the sled," George said. "Paddy drove, and I ran alongside and threw out the hay, so he didn't have to walk so much."

"Thank you. It's good to know that I can trust you all to do the jobs when I'm not here." She looked across the room. Paddy stared solemnly at her, his bony face long and dejected.

She blinked hard and smiled at him. "He'll be fine,

Paddy. The hospital is looking after him, and I'm sure he'll be home in no time. Now, let's get this table set so I can dish up our meal. Timmy, would you run and see if the men have finished washing yet?"

By the time everyone had finished eating, there was not a crust or crumb left.

"Good cook." Grant wiped his mouth and looked at Alice. She was certain that, had she not been watching, he would have licked his bowl. As it was, there was no trace of the steamed pudding and cream that had filled the plate minutes before.

She poured the hot tea into cups and passed them around the table before turning to the sink. Her head spun, and she gripped the bench. She was tired, worried, and she wished everyone would hurry up and go to bed so she could be alone.

―――――

Fantail Ridge
South Head
26 June 1938

Dear Maud,

I hope you are all well and received my previous letter?

It looks as though it will be some time before Harry comes home. He developed blood poisoning and didn't respond well to the drugs they put him on. However, I telephoned the matron yesterday, and she said he seems better now due to a change of medication. He apparently ate a little bit of his tea last night, which is always a good sign.

When I got home from Helensville the other day, the plumbers were here and then the builders turned up the following morning, together with the painters. Thank goodness. I think I will be a raving lunatic if I have to cater for a heap of men in this shed much longer! I am so looking forward to being able to cook in my new kitchen, with benches and proper cupboards and a place for everything. Not long now though. I haven't told any of the workmen that Harry is taking so long to recover. A bit naughty of me, I know, but I want them to think Harry could be back any minute so they hurry up and finish! It will be wonderful to move in when he gets home. The painters estimate another ten to twelve days—weather permitting—and they will be the last ones to leave.

Thankfully, it hasn't rained much this week—just a shower or two, so progress has been good.

I'm desperate to visit Harry again but can't leave while there are so many mouths to feed. Harry would understand. Clive called in yesterday and kindly waited while I wrote Harry a quick note. He said he would pop in and visit him and deliver it for me in person. He's such a nice young man and was heading into town to visit a girl. It seems he has his eye on a young lady from up Dargaville way. They met at a dance somewhere, and once a month she comes to Helensville by boat to visit her aunt. I gather the aunt must approve! Not sure what Vince thinks though as they both used to go to town together. He (Vince that is) came to have tea with us all last night, but with so many here, I didn't get to talk to him.

You will laugh—I have altered a pair of Harry's trousers so I can wear them on the farm. I'm going to help with the stock work until Harry is well enough, and riding in a skirt is so uncomfortable. As soon as some of the workers leave, Paddy, the boys, and I are mustering the sheep and will draft out the rams. I haven't been on a horse for so long so hope I don't fall off! Poor Paddy has a lot of pain in his hips and legs now and is unable to ride. He says walking is easier. I'll let you know how I get on.

I look forward to hearing from you soon. I know you will have written, so perhaps this week will bring me all your news? I'll nip down to the wharf now and see if I can catch Ed to post this.

Lots of love to you all,

Alice

"I'm taking letters to Ed's to go in the post. Do you want to come?" Alice called to John as he ran past the window, shrieking with laughter with Flossie hard on his heels. He stopped abruptly, and the dog almost crashed into him.

With the exception of John and Flossie, the only sounds were the occasional bleating of sheep and the trees sighing in the wind. Even the banging in the new house had stopped and Alice hoped that was a good sign?

After lunch, George and Timmy had gone to the lake halfway across the farm to catch tadpoles. The lake was more like a large pond really, and Alice wasn't at all sure that frogs even spawned in winter. However, it gave the older boys something to do on a Sunday afternoon and, in many ways, she envied them. Paddy had taken himself off to have a lie down in his little cabin, cursing under his breath about arthritis. Alice had overheard him grumbling so had given him a couple of Aspirin and happily waved him away with as much sympathy as she could muster.

What she really wanted to do was to visit Harry.

"I'm coming." John was panting, his face a rosy pink.

Alice pulled a knitted wool hat over her hair and buttoned up her coat. She slipped her letter to Maud into her pocket next to the one she had written to Harry. She had so much to tell him and had sat up late the previous night, pouring her thoughts, her questions, and her love onto the paper under the light of a kerosene lamp.

———

"Hello. Are you here, Ed?"

Rhythmic slaps of the incoming waves beat against the dingy tied to the edge of the wharf. The little boat bobbed and swayed, pulling against its tether as a seagull screamed above.

Alice narrowed her eyes against the wind and gazed around the dwelling. There was no sign of life. The door was closed, its frame rattling against the prevailing wind. Even the window in the old shack was dull and unwelcoming, its privacy curtain a thick coating of salt spray.

"I'll go and see if he's in the garden, Mum?" John didn't wait for Alice to answer, racing out of sight with Flossie at his heels.

Toetoe and clumps of flax waved and rustled in the breeze. Shivers ran up Alice's spine, and she rubbed her upper arms.

About to call John, something dark farther around the foreshore caught her eye. It was shaped like a hut but well camouflaged, as a bird-watching hide might be, and covered with large fern leaves and tea tree. *I'm certain that wasn't there last time I came down?*

The little boy reappeared as her heart beat harder.

"Nope. He's not there," John said.

Alice patted Flossie lightly on the head.

"Come on. We're going to see what that is." She pointed, clutching John's hand tightly as she stepped off the wharf and onto the narrow, muddy track that wove its way around the shoreline.

As they drew closer, the sound of a hammer on steel caught on the wind, greeting the explorers. Alice flinched as it crashed again, louder this time.

"Hello!" She cupped her hands around her mouth to prevent her call from being blown away and started when Ed stepped out of the hide to face them. He wiped his hands on a rag, and a glimmer of a smile hovered around his mouth.

"Oh hello, Ed. I have some mail for you to put on the boat tonight please?"

Curious, John pointed to the source of the noise. "Whatcha doing in there, Mr Ed?"

"Come see." He turned his back, and John shot Alice a quick glance before running after him. Following the big man and tiny boy, Alice screwed up her nose. Smoke, oil, and something earthy greeted them, and her eyes widened as she adjusted to the dark.

The hut was sturdier than she'd first realised and housed an array of steel, tools, and an anvil similar to the one in the blacksmith's where her father's horses were shod many years ago. She stared at the contraption sitting on a slab of timber. "Is that our engine? The one that drives our shearing plant?"

Ed nodded sheepishly. "Harry asked me to send to town on the boat. I knew I could fix it. So I did. He's a good man."

Alice opened her mouth and then shut it again. She was unsure if he was referring to himself or Harry, and as that was the longest speech she had ever heard him give, she wasn't sure how to respond. As far as they knew, Ed was a simple man who lived in a shack by the beach and in return for being allowed to live on the narrow piece of foreshore that seemed to belong to nobody, kept a few stores for the locals and grew vegetables to accompany the fish he caught.

"Are you an engineer of some sort? Or a blacksmith?"

He shrugged.

For a minute they studied each other, and then he slapped the side of his head. "I don't know."

"What do you mean you don't know?"

"I don't know what I am."

He turned back to the engine and wiped it with his rag.

"I will bring it back to shed tomorrow and make it work."

Alice blinked, torn between cross-questioning this strange man or keeping her mouth shut until Harry got home. He would know what to say—that is, if there was anything to say? She dug in her pocket and held out the letters. "Would you please send these on the boat tonight?"

"Ya." He took a clean piece of rag from his pocket and carefully wound it around his dirty hand before grasping Alice's letters.

"Thank you." Alice hesitated and smiled. Then she grabbed John's arm and hurried back towards the road.

As they toiled up the hill to Fantail Ridge, she barely heard John's chatter or Flossie's snuffling as she inspected rabbit holes on the banks of the road.

Ya? What country does Ed come from? And why would someone with obvious knowledge of machinery hide away in a hut and live almost solely from the land and sea?

It didn't make sense, and Alice could barely wait until Wednesday when she planned to visit Harry again.

CHAPTER 17

Alice twitched her nose and took a deep breath before walking through the front door of the hospital. This time she was prepared for the onslaught of disinfectant. Instead, she was pleasantly surprised to be greeted by the scent of lavender drifting in the air, slightly suppressing the smells of methylated spirits and something she didn't recognise. The building oozed not just cleanliness, but a calm comfort, and Matron's familiar face in the corridor was a welcome sight.

"Good afternoon, Mrs Simpson. He is so much better today. If your husband continues to improve at this rate, you'll be taking him home next week."

Alice's heart leapt. *Really? Only one more week?* She thanked Matron and hurried towards the ward.

His face was so thin and pale, Alice bent quickly to kiss him in an attempt to hide her shock.

"I got your letter." He squeezed her hand and smiled. "We've got lots to talk about."

Delight surged through her and she chuckled. "We have. Starting with what I am supposed to do with the rams?"

"Leave them until I get home. Paddy and the boys can help sort them out."

Alice rolled her eyes. She'd have to handle her questions more delicately than she thought—she didn't have to be a doctor to see that it would be weeks before he would be strong enough to return to normal farm duties.

"We'll put the rams in your park so they can clean up the grass before spring, and then the daffodils will be enjoyed by everyone driving past." Harry grinned at her. "What do you think?"

"I agree. I planted another few clumps last week. I know it's a bit late, but I'm hoping that by September the hill will be a sea of yellow and cream." She shuffled her feet, a little self-conscious of the smug pride she had for her precious park.

Irene had given her three trees—a flame, a kowhai, and a totara, and in the warm, well-drained soil of late summer, all had already reached the top of their protective chicken wire surrounds. For Alice, they were a nice mix to complement the Norfolk pine and eucalypt that she had nurtured for the past three years. Her dream was to stabilise the steep, triangular-shaped paddock on the side of the hill and create an area of beauty that would last long after both she and Harry had turned to dust.

The time flew as Alice clung to Harry's hand while they talked and laughed—companionably, softly, barely taking their eyes off one another. Their love for each other was strong and true, and neither illness nor accident should have been needed to remind her of that. It had, however, given them both a shock that they would not forget in a hurry.

The bell signalling the end of visiting hours clanged down the hall, startling Alice, and she jumped. She straightened Harry's bedcover and gathered up the pile of newspapers from the bedside table. Smiling, she touched the flowers in the vase, the happy faces of the pansies and the pinks and purples of the fuchsia flowers so similar to a troupe of miniature ballerinas. On her way out, she snatched up the spent, drooping bunch that had taken pride of place on the windowsill and deposited them in the rubbish bin.

A fading autumn sun greeted her as she emerged from the hospital, and her plans began to form as she drove past the thermal baths and accelerated towards home.

———

ALICE UNTIED HER APRON AND HUNG IT ON THE HOOK behind the door. She wore a flannelette blouse, a jersey she had knitted a decade ago, and a pair of Harry's khaki trousers, firmly held around her waist by a narrow leather belt.

Paddy and the boys wolfed down their breakfast and left to catch the horses while Alice cleaned up the kitchen and gave the floor a cursory sweep. Then she pulled on her boots and jacket and tucked a loose lock of hair under the woollen hat.

Outside, Saturday dawned with one of those glorious winter skies, pale blue streaked with pink rays of the rising sun as it crept slowly over the horizon. A family of magpies warbled as they sat on the top wire of the fence, and Alice blew a long breath of white mist and grinned.

"Good morning, my feathered friends."

The sea was quiet and the tide low, exposing vast expanses of mud and sand. Shadowy puddles dotted the tidal flats, and the air was fresh and still. Alive with purpose, and anticipating Harry's homecoming in a few days' time, she marched towards the woolshed.

"You'll have to ride Blaze, Mum." At George's anxious announcement, Alice laughed.

"Thank you. I'm sure we'll get along well. Won't we, Blaze?" She fondled the horse's ears and stared him in the eye. *I'm putting my trust in you.*

She leaned through the open door of the woolshed and reached for the pair of old pigskin gloves she kept on the shelf. Their familiar cool softness touched her hand and she grabbed them, raised her eyes, and froze. No longer vacant, the corner where the shearing engine had been prior to its breakdown had been empty for weeks, and she had grown used to the empty space. Now the contraption that sat in its position looked similar, except it was painted red, displayed a shiny new starter button, and was very, very clean. She moved closer to it, and her eyes widened. It was their original, but it looked brand new. *How on earth did Ed get it in here on his own?*

Still filled with amazement, she led Blaze to the yards and climbed the railing before sliding relatively elegantly onto the saddle.

George had fastened a thick hessian sack over Duke's back, held in place with a surcingle. He scrambled onboard the patient animal and hauled John up behind him.

"I'll do the gates," Timmy said. He rode Stormy, proudly upright in the child's saddle, its girth buckled tightly around the pony's chubby belly.

Once again, Paddy chose to walk. He had equipped himself with a sturdy stick to lean on and in the other hand, carried his treacle tin. Around his neck hung a sheep whistle on a leather thong. Concern for the man absorbed Alice's attention, and her gaze followed him as he trudged across the paddock.

"Will he be alright, Mum?" George whispered.

"I hope so. We'll do our best to look after him."

George nodded and urged Duke into a brisk walk while Blaze strode out behind. John clung to his brother, his arms wrapped around George's waist, giggling at Timmy bouncing up and down like a dingy on the ocean as Stormy jig-jogged alongside them. Rock and Flossie fanned out behind the procession, alert and energetic.

They crossed the creek that flowed from a spring at the top end of the farm and broke into a trot as the paddock rose in front of them. A piercing whistle floated across the land. Alice sought the origins of the sound, surprised to see Paddy leaning on his stick on the brow of the next hill. Rock streaked past them and made a wide sweep around the flock spreading across the slopes. As he worked back and forth, a cream river of sheep flowed down the paddock and into the valley.

"George, you go that way, and Timmy and I'll go along the ridge and bring the mob from the far paddock." Alice pointed to a wide-open area surrounded by pine trees and dotted with grazing stock.

The animals raised their heads as the riders approached, then while the cattle remained stationery, the sheep clustered together, swirling in an anxious circle. "You won't have any trouble with that lot. Hang on tight, John."

The boys grinned at her, and Duke carried them away at a brisk walk.

"Come on, Timmy. We've got a job to do." Alice led the way as they climbed, single file, up a narrow, muddy sheep track. Leaning forward in the saddle, a smile played around her mouth. *Thank goodness I didn't follow my elder sisters. Being a genteel country wife, enter-taining all the time, and never venturing around the perimeter of their farms would not be much help to me now.*

Reaching the top of the rise, they looked across to where sheep spread over the paddock and dotted the steep hill at the northern end. Alice gulped. It had been a long time since she'd ridden this far, and already her thighs and lower back were aching. She couldn't see Paddy or Duke anywhere and hoped they hadn't met with a mishap of some sort.

"Beat you to the top, Mum." Timmy flapped his legs and bent over the pony's neck as Stormy broke into a scrambling gait that resembled a half-hearted gallop. They rode towards the fence-line, and Alice let Blaze have his head. Her smile grew as she adjusted to the gentle rocking motion of his canter, and the wind kissed her cheeks.

In almost three years of living on Fantail Ridge, she had explored every inch of their land, mostly on foot with John. Those exploratory walks gave her an advantage she hadn't considered at the time.

Blaze jumped sideways, and Alice clutched a handful of mane and shuffled herself back into the saddle. Her heart pounded as his ears pricked up and she turned. In a flash of black and tan, Flossie thundered from behind them and galloped straight up the steep slope, her head stretched forward and her stride as long as a horse's. She barked—a deep, deafening sound that echoed across the hills and had the sheep bounding away in terror.

Timmy pulled Stormy to a halt, and Alice gladly reined Blaze in to stand beside him, watching in awe as Flossie raced along the ridge to the opposite side of the paddock. In all the time she had lived with them, the dog had never shown any interest in the stock—or any other animal for that matter. Now it was as though a switch had been tripped in her brain and she understood exactly what had to be done.

"Look at them go." Timmy bounced around on the pony's back while Stormy dropped his head and snatched mouthfuls of grass.

Sheep rushed down the hill and leapt across the creek before joining a second flock emerging from behind the scrub. They milled together in the valley like an incoming tide. From her position on the hilltop, Alice squinted, picking out the lone, bent figure of Paddy and the sandy-coloured dog trotting at his heels. They crossed the valley floor behind the stragglers and herded them up the other side towards the woolshed.

With no sign of George and John, Alice scanned every direction, her chest tightening. The folds in the land between where she stood and the direction Duke had headed were covered with tea tree, and along the ridge, a number of small bluffs glistened, their golden walls scars overlooking the land below. Alice took comfort in the knowledge that a formed stock track wound its way to the boys' destination. They needed only to open gates before riding around behind the sheep, and if they took it slowly, the animals would congregate in a tight mob that moved as one towards their friends.

A long breath hissed slowly from her lips when she spotted the faithful bay gelding plodding behind a thick flock of ewes and rams, his cargo of one tall and one small boy casually pointing to something in a tree as their voices carried across the valley.

Three mobs of sheep melted into one as they approached the woolshed, and once again, Alice's delight grew as the big Huntaway swept back and forth, instinctively keeping them tightly together. Flossie's awakening and the long, frustrating days Harry had spent building fences in a pattern made for easy stock management. Alice beamed. Her job had been easier than she'd thought.

The riders trailed the last sheep through the final gate and waited while Paddy closed it firmly behind them.

Dismounting quickly, the boys' attention was consumed by the penned sheep before Alice kicked her feet out of the stirrups and swung her leg over the saddle. She slithered down the horse's side, hanging on to the pommel and talking softly to Blaze. It took a minute or more before the numbness eased and she trusted her legs to move without collapsing.

"What a gentleman you are. Thank you for under-standing and treating me so well."

Blaze turned his head and nudged her, and she smiled at the horses.

"You gallant steeds can have a rest now. We're taking a break and will be back."

———

LUNCH WAS A WELCOME, UNHURRIED AFFAIR, AND ALICE was glad she had pushed herself in the kitchen the previous day and accomplished more than normal. Vegetable soup with fresh-baked bread was followed with apple pie and custard, washed down with gallons of hot tea.

"The custard tastes funny, Mum." Timmy licked his lips and frowned. "Are we on milk powder again?"

"Afraid so. Josie needs a rest. I stocked up with butter last week, and you'll have to adjust to having powdered milk for a few weeks."

With only a month to go before she calved again, the cow had been dried off and moved to a sheltered paddock beyond the house yard.

"Boys, will you clear the table please, and then you can go with Paddy? I'll be down as soon as I've washed up here." Alice glanced out the window at the two dogs lying in the sun on the lawn as she waited for the sink to fill.

"Wasn't Flossie amazing?" She turned to Paddy and shook her head. "I wonder what happened to make her suddenly remember what a Huntaway is supposed to do. Instinct?"

Paddy cleared his throat and shrugged. "If she could talk, I s'pose she'd tell us."

The old man mooched steadily across the yard while the children fooled around, playing with the dogs as they went.

He looks done in. She hurriedly dried the final plate and hung up the tea towel.

Ramming her feet back into her boots, she flinched, the muscles in her back protesting. Massaging her lumber area as she moved, she followed them to the yards and steeled herself for a tough afternoon.

In the end, it wasn't as gruelling as she had expected. With the boys pushing the sheep into the race, aided by Rock and Flossie, and she and Paddy operating the drafting gates, they methodically checked every animal, separating the ewes from the rams as they went.

Shadows lay across the paddock, and the evening stilled as the ewes trickled into their new paddock, fanning out as they flowed onto the green pasture.

"Enjoy yourselves, ladies. The boys won't be bothering you now." Alice grinned and returned to the yards, sighing with relief as she faced the pen full of rams. *Last job for the day.*

Surrounded by Paddy, Alice, and the boys, and with the dogs weaving studiously back and forth behind them, the small flock strolled from the woolshed towards the house, crossed the road onto the lawn, and were urged briskly past the new garden. The white picket gate beside the puriri tree glistened in the fading light, and the rams ran through the opening and down the steep, east-facing slope into knee-deep grass.

Alice dropped the wire loop over the post and turned to gaze at the new house. Final rays of winter sun hovered on the horizon, silhouetting the silent, fully completed dwelling, and blood pumped through her veins, filling her with hope and delight.

Tomorrow they would begin to move in.

CHAPTER 18

Excitement resonated through the rooms as bedding was rolled and boxes filled. Alice, Paddy, and the boys trekked back and forth between the house and the make-do shed that had been their home for over two and a half years. They stacked belongings into the cupboards and carefully manoeuvred furniture through the widest doorways into position.

She had wavered over shifting the beds, deciding they would not sleep in the new house until Harry came home, but the boys, unable to contain their excitement, pointed out that it would be a wonderful surprise for their father if he arrived home to find the work had been done.

Vince and Clive came for tea on Sunday night, and as Alice showed them through the new house and they shared the family's enthusiasm, arrangements were made for their return early on Wednesday morning, bringing an extra man or two with them.

They duly arrived, reassuring Alice the solid double bed, piano, and heavy kitchen table would be in place by the time she returned with Harry. Rugs, a couch, and armchairs that had been stored under layers of sheets and canvas in the machinery shed were unwrapped and sat in the sun to air prior to being installed no later than mid-afternoon.

Her heart sang—almost as loudly as her voice as she drove to Helensville. Feverish with anticipation, she raced up the main street, leaving the food order with the grocer while she visited the Post Office, completed their banking, and picked up the curtain material from the drapers.

On the dot of two o'clock, she pushed open the hospital door and hurried to greet her husband.

Alice threw her arms around him, almost knocking him off his feet before standing back and taking a good, long look at the man she loved. "You look wonderful." She disregarded his pallor and thin frame now. They were incidental, and she would ensure that with her cooking and time spent outdoors again, he would be back to his old self in no time.

"Not as good as you, my love." He kissed her before whispering, "Get me out of here."

Leaning heavily on Alice, Harry waved goodbye to the other patients, thanked the matron and nurse, and hobbled outside to the car.

They wound up and down each hill and steadily traversed the straight sections of road while all the way, Harry's head pivoted left and right, as though unable to soak up enough of the countryside. He talked more than Alice could ever remember—until they reached the flat leading to Fantail Ridge. Then, for the last mile, Harry sat in complete silence, his eyes firmly fixed on their new house while Alice negotiated the steep, twisting turns of the final hill.

They swung into the yard, and she gasped at the crowd gathered in front of the shed. She switched off the engine and stared, immobile. Their boys, the Bennett family, Clive and Vince, their new neighbours, the McDonalds from over the next hill that they had only met once, and of course Paddy and the dogs were waiting to greet them.

She slid out of the driver's seat, stretching her diminutive physique to a new height, and her smile grew while the boys hauled Harry's door open and scrambled to hug him first.

After all the hand-shaking and hugging ended, Alice took Harry's arm and led him through the gate, along the narrow path, and up the porch steps to the door of their home.

He stopped and shook his head gently, as though he couldn't believe what he was seeing. Inside, Irene's touches were everywhere. Vases of greenery and tiny sprays of pansies stood on the table, windowsills, and a narrow, wooden stand in the entrance hall that Alice had forgotten they owned. The beautiful, cream-coloured wood stove dominated the kitchen, and inside its belly, a fire crackled and shared its warmth. Two large pots sat on the hob, one filled with an aromatic stew and the other with enough potatoes to feed a small army.

"Is this our home?" Harry smiled and sat in the antique, sculpted chair that had been his grandfather's and was too bulky to use in the shed kitchen. "I think you'd all better stay and join us for tea."

Everyone laughed and, although they didn't all stay, the Bennetts, Clive, and Vince did, leaving only after the last dish was washed, dried, and placed in the cupboard.

It was pitch dark when Alice turned down the lamp and slipped into bed. She wrapped her arms around her husband and snuggled against him. Outside their bedroom, perched on a branch in the puriri tree, a morepork called, and a sense of peace settled over the homestead.

Fantail Ridge
South Head
10 July 1938

Dear Maud,

He's home! I'm so relieved and happy—and very grateful to the doctor and nurses at the hospital. To top it off, we are in our new house!

Thank you for the pile of letters (I collected them from the post office on Wednesday).

We managed to get everything moved into the house before I got home with Harry, thanks to the help of our wonderful friends. Irene had filled every vase with whatever plant life she could find and made enough stew and spuds to feed a troupe of soldiers—it was a lovely thought, and we all had a great evening.

Harry is tired and pale, but gets up at dawn each morning and goes outside. Being locked in the hospital for weeks has been harder for him than coping with an injury, so even when it's raining, he's out pottering in the shed or wandering around the farm with the dogs and his walking stick. At least his leg is healing nicely, and he says within a few weeks, he'll be walking normally again (I hope so).

I must tell you something that happened yesterday though. When Paddy came in for lunch, he was really morose and seemed to have something on his mind. The only word he said was 'thank you' when he left. Anyway, Harry went down to the woolshed during the afternoon and found him sitting on a wool bale staring into space, so he stayed with him for a couple of hours. He was obviously depressed about something, then, (according to Harry), Paddy just started talking and didn't stop for ages. He said he knows he is not physically capable to help Harry as he would like to anymore and has been worrying about what will become of him. He's terrified of ending up in an institution just like when he was a foundling in that ghastly place in Ireland as a child. Isn't it awful? Poor man. I know some of our family have never trusted him, but I'll bet if they had lived his life they would think differently.

Now that we are in the house, we have moved Paddy out of the shepherd's hut and into our 'temporary accommodation' (i.e. the shed). He loves having access to the old stove out there, and even though he still joins us for meals, he can make a hot drink or whatever he wants, the room is nice and warm during winter, and the wash house and outside toilet are handy for him.

I think Harry has convinced him there's no point wanting to die as he's now part of our family and has a home with us forever. We've also rearranged the shearer's room so it can be used for any workmen who come. It's got a set of bunks, two single beds, and two wooden fruit boxes that serve as bedside tables.

Phew! That's about all from here. I hope the family are well.

Lots of love to you all,
Alice

———

WITH HIS LEG STILL TOO PAINFUL TO DO MUCH FARM work, Harry suggested they harness Duke, pack the billy and this morning's leftover scones, and head to the beach. The air was cold and clear after the previous day's rain, and the land sparkled under the pale winter sun.

Alice tucked the letter to Maud in her pocket and picked up the basket. The six of them squeezed together in the crowded buggy and Alice shook the reins. Duke tossed his head, leaned into the traces, and twitched an ear at his mistress's command to walk on.

On their arrival at the foot of the hill, her gaze rested on the tall, solemn man in the distance. In front of his shack, he remained motionless, seemingly absorbed by their approach. Even after all this time, Alice was uncertain of him.

Perhaps she was a little afraid? Why? He seemed generous and surprisingly clever. After all, hadn't he repaired their engine without being asked? And Irene had said only last week that he had offered to teach her children how to row a boat properly after, apparently, catching sight of three of them floundering around in the water. He had told Jack he was concerned they didn't have the skills to manage the battered dingy they were in, especially if a squall blew through.

George got out to open the gate, and Alice glanced at Harry. His face was pink, and his eyes sparkled. Five days out of hospital and he was clearly on the road to recovery. She leaned over and kissed his cheek. A fantail flittered amongst the giant flax bushes before perching on the highest stem, peering at them.

"What are you doing here, little bird?" Alice smiled.

certainly had advantages—nevertheless, the sense of isolation clawed from time to time.

John was now at school, and she sighed as she looked around the room. The only advantage of his absence was to provide more opportunities to cook, sew, and garden without interruption.

She screwed the lids on the bottles of plum sauce and set them aside while she scrubbed the preserving pot. A leg of mutton and bread and butter pudding were slowly cooking in the wood oven, and she glanced at the clock. If she hurried, she would have time to walk through the bush and meet the boys at the bottom of the hill. The older two didn't say much, but John welcomed his mother's company while walking home from school.

Flossie staggered to her feet, her heavily pregnant belly rolling as she lumbered alongside her mistress. In the distance, Alice glimpsed Harry tilling the hayshed paddock. It had been his goal this week—to sow new seed while the ground was warm. He followed Duke and the plough across the light brown soil, and an anxious smile hovered around Alice's mouth. Harry had reassured her the walking strengthened his leg, and at this time of year, with the weather neither too hot nor cold, it was perfect for planting.

She scrambled down the track and slowed to a gentle stroll where the bush opened up and the fantails flittered back and forth in the cool dampness.

A group of children hovered over the bridge rails

above the creek, throwing sticks in and rushing from side to side. Alice grinned. Their journey home varied from twenty minutes to over an hour, depending on the tide and the weather. In spite of the McDonald children having to walk over five miles home, what was a few extra minutes spent playing with water on a lovely day like this?

"Hello, Mrs Simpson!" The youngest McDonald, Archie, was the first to catch sight of her, and he waved frantically.

She waved back and called, "Hello".

As quick as lightning, Timmy dropped something into the stream, and Alice frowned. Was that a puff of smoke? A cigarette? *You little rascal—you're smoking.* As she covered the final few yards to the road, she decided to ignore it, for the moment anyway. Occasionally, Harry smoked a pipe, and most of the men she knew regularly dragged on cigarettes, but the thought of her own boys smoking had never occurred to her. *He is still at primary school.*

———

TEN DAYS LATER, FLOSSIE GAVE BIRTH TO EIGHT FAT puppies. Half the litter were black and tan and the other half, a sandy colour like their father, with a hint of a dark shadow across their backs. While shielding the pups from Rock and the boys, Flossie allowed Alice to move them to a clean, dry bed in the boot room. The day after their birth, the weather broke, and an early winter surged in with a vengeance. The windows in the house were peppered with heavy rain, driven by the howling wind. The pine trees, now over twelve feet tall, swayed and sighed, and Flossie snuggled her babies against her while Rock eyed her warily and squeezed as close as possible to the warmth generated by the motor of the kerosene fridge.

"Just got the paddock sown in time." Harry hovered in the doorway, peering into the sodden sheets as they fell from the sky and flowed in a shallow river across the lawn. "Hope it doesn't wash the seed away."

"Don't be gloomy," Alice chided. "Winter might have arrived early but if we didn't get rain everyone would be complaining." She came up behind him and leaned on his shoulder. "I love it. It's like a magic potion for the soil, and everything is always so clean and fresh afterwards."

Harry put his arm over her shoulders and chuckled. "Such a romantic."

"No I'm not. I'm being practical." She dug him in the ribs. "Come on. You said you were going to catch up with the accounts next time it was too wet to do anything outside. Here's your chance."

"Let's have a cuppa first."

Alice grinned and went back inside to fill the kettle.

Half the table was covered with a jigsaw puzzle and, to Alice's surprise, George and Timmy were bent over the project, without argument, silent with concentration. Perhaps it was the rain, or perhaps it was simply that they were growing up. "Great work, boys."

George looked up briefly while Timmy put another piece in place.

"Where's John?" Only minutes before he had been annoying his older brothers, and Alice had felt more like a referee in a football match than a mother.

"He's gone to see Paddy." Timmy shook his head as he spoke, and Alice grinned.

"Of course."

Flossie's possessiveness over her puppies had confused the little boy, and she was pleased that Paddy had become his choice when he wanted company.

As Harry stood beside her, Alice stared out of the kitchen window across to Paddy's room. The two of them were sitting on either side of the wood stove in the shed, and in spite of the rain, John's blond head was visible, bent towards the open book on Paddy's lap.

Alice's monthly sojourns to town included a visit to the library before heading home to choose books for Paddy. Most times, she and the librarian were able to find something from his list of suggestions. However, lately the number of classics and mysteries were reducing and stories more suited to children, increasing. *Black Beauty*, *The Cat Who Went to Heaven*, and *Bright Island* were the current choices, and from the brief glimpses through the window, both man and boy were entranced.

"He really is like a grandfather to the boys, isn't he?"

"I suppose he is in a way," Harry said. "He seems to enjoy spending time with them as much as they do him. And I, for one, am grateful for the patience he's shown and all the things he's taught them over the years."

"Hmm. Me too. I wonder which one of them will use their skills in horsemanship and leatherwork as the years go by. Will they become farmers too? Or will they take a completely different path?"

Harry turned to face Alice as she spoke, and she blinked at the surprise on his face. "I presume they will all become farmers. That's one of the reasons we moved here—to give them the opportunity."

"I know. But we mustn't force them into farming if their hearts take them elsewhere. You know how upset you were when your father gave you no option but to be a dairy farmer. It was not your choice, and we have all worked very hard to make the change. Anyway, none of us knows what their future will be, especially now there's a possibility of another war." Alice stopped short, uncertain which of them was more surprised at her outburst.

Ever since reading Maud's letter, the suggestion of another war had disturbed her. Now she studied Harry's troubled expression and her fear grew.

"Is it true then?" she whispered. "There is going to be another war?"

"I don't know, but I thank God every single night

that our boys are too young to fight. Not sure about me though."

Bile rose in Alice's throat, and her legs threatened to give way. She clutched the edge of the sink. *No, no, no. One war in anyone's life is one too many. Please don't let it happen again?*

CHAPTER 20

5 September 1939

ALICE, HARRY, AND PADDY SAT PERCHED ON THE EDGE of their chairs, listening intently as the radio crackled and squealed. Harry jumped up and adjusted the knobs, while across the hall behind the dark-panelled door, the boys slept, unaware of the news that had disturbed their parents so intensely two days prior. The static stopped briefly, and the voice of Michael Savage, New Zealand's Prime Minister, rang clearly through the room.

"It is with gratitude in the past, and with confidence in the future, that we range ourselves without fear beside Britain. Where she goes, we go. Where she stands, we stand."

Alice heard no more. Fear occupied her, and she swallowed hard.

"That's that then," Harry said.

"What will it mean for us? Will you be called up? Do you have to volunteer?" Alice's voice was barely audible.

Harry reached over and squeezed her hand. "It'll be alright, love. I'm sure it will all blow over in no time, and we'll have nothing to worry about."

A heaviness within her prevented movement, and it was a long time before she rose for bed.

———

Fantail Ridge
South Head
1 December 1939

DEAR MAUD,

We are looking forward to seeing you all here on Fantail Ridge for Christmas. With the war and so many of our boys being deployed overseas, it appears we don't know what will happen in the new year, so we must make the most of these special occasions while we can.

I feel a bit guilty admitting my relief that Harry is not expected to join up again. Thank goodness the provision of food is considered important enough for our men to remain at home with us. I imagine Dougal is also involved in the Home Guard though? I actually think Harry will enjoy the company even though it's for such an essential purpose—a purpose for which I dearly hope will not be needed. I'm also grateful that our children are too young to be involved.

I received a long letter from Harry's sister, Nancy, last week, and she is quite bereft after waving goodbye to their Phillip. Being their only child, I imagine she would feel the emptiness even more than we would, especially as he's only seventeen. She said he's in training at the moment, and his troupe are being despatched soon, but she doesn't know to where.

Meanwhile, life continues as normal here. I hope Flossie's pup is turning out well for you all. We were a bit surprised how easy it was finding homes for them, but both Vince and Clive are delighted with how good their dogs are with stock. If Flossie and Rock have another litter, I suspect we will receive orders for them. It seems a bit odd that they (Rock and Flossie) have never really been great friends, but they certainly produced beautiful offspring. Maybe it's because Rock has always been Harry's dog, whereas Flossie is more attached to the boys and me.

The shearers are due again next week, so I have been baking frantically and trying to prepare for Christmas as well. The puddings and fruit cakes are made, and Harry has put two legs of mutton in the smoker. It's very tasty (much like ham) and keeps better than the fresh meat. George is getting quite keen on shooting, and he and Sam Bennett have said they will knock over a couple of geese from Bennett's flock for us for Christmas as well. They (Bennetts, I mean) are having some of their own family this year, so it will just be us (including Paddy, of course) and possibly Vince. He has plans to go to Auckland if the weather and workload permit. Clive and his girl are engaged now, so Clive will be spending Christmas with her family.

I finally finished the summer dress I started a month ago and hope Christmas day is warm enough for me to wear it. I've also used the last of the gaberdine fabric I bought a couple of years ago, to make trousers for myself and the boys. They are so practical on the farm, especially for riding.

Speaking of riding, I'm enclosing a letter to Dougal from Harry with this. He's hoping Dougal will be able to find us another horse (or two) as Duke is slowing down and although he's still great to ride or to pull the buggy, he struggles with the sled and plough. We really need a heavy horse like one of your Clydesdales. There is talk of petrol being restricted if the ships can't get here, so it seems that we may have to rely on the horses more than the truck and car?

I have made your boys a shirt each and also a blouse with little puffed sleeves for Catherine. I hope they will like them. When you drive through Riverhead on the way here, would you please stop at the orchard and pick up a box of fruit for me? I will give you the money when you get here. We were hoping to go ourselves, but with the shearers coming, I doubt we'll have time.

I had better get on now. Josie is producing heaps of milk at the moment, so I'm making butter every second day. The chooks are also laying well and the vegetables coming on quickly, so we have to be grateful for small mercies.

Can't wait to see you all. Take care and give Catherine a special hug from me. Can you believe Emmie would be turning seven next month if she was still with us? Our children are growing up fast, but she will forever be my baby.

Until Christmas—my love to you all,
Alice

———

"I'M JUST GOING TO PICK ED UP." HARRY'S VOICE carried from the end of the boot room at the same time as Alice pulled two loaves of fresh bread from the oven.

"What for?" she called back.

"He said he'll come and check the shearing engine works properly before the team get started tomorrow."

She removed her hands from the oven mitts and stood in the kitchen doorway. "Oh. Bring him up for lunch if you like. I know he'll probably refuse, but you never know?"

Harry grinned. "Righto. I can try, anyway." He turned away, and Alice listened for the click of the gate latch before returning to the stove.

Over the years, she couldn't count the number of times they had issued invitations to Ed. It was pointless. His answer was always a polite thank you and a shake of his head. Nevertheless, Alice had been brought up to be hospitable, and even if he was an enigma, to her he was still Ed—their reliable storekeeper and mailman—and she would not give him the chance to think she didn't appreciate his services.

It was Wednesday and the final week of school for

the boys. The weather was cool and blustery, dousing everyone's high hopes of an early summer. So far, it hadn't eventuated, but Harry regularly stated optimistically, *there's always tomorrow.*

With the weekly washing strung across the cow paddock and the cooking up to date, Alice sat on the sofa next to a basket full of mending. She turned the radio on, pulled a sock over the wooden mushroom, and began to weave the wool needle back and forth across the hole.

The news bulletin had begun, and Alice was listening intently when a crash and a man's voice sounded outside, startling her. Someone had entered the house yard. She frowned. Deep tones, certainly not belonging to Harry, drifted through the open window. Dropping her mending, she hurried to the door.

Caught off guard, she smiled while her eyes opened wide. "Hello, Ed."

Harry stood back and waved the man inside. Next to their visitor, Harry's slight, wiry figure appeared childlike, and Alice shrank against the bench as the big man filled the room.

"Please, sit down. Alice will make us tea." Harry pulled out a chair and sat directly opposite him.

Alice bustled about, placing bread, cold meat, pickles, and fresh plums on the table before filling the teapot. "It's great having enough space to invite people in now. It was always so crowded in the shed, and we tripped over one another. Would you like milk in your tea?" Alice babbled on while Burl Ives's dulcet tones resonated from deep within the radio.

Ed nodded in silence, and a shadow of a smile touched the corners of his mouth.

"Ed's got the shearing plant running better than it ever has … Well, since we've been here, anyway," Harry said.

"Wonderful. Thank you, Ed." She paused for a couple of seconds. "Were you always a man with many talents?"

He stared at her with eyes the colour of the ocean and their depths as mysterious. The air seemed to thicken, and Alice's heart thumped. She'd said something wrong.

It seemed like an age, but in fact it was only seconds before he responded. "I don't know. I can't remember anything. I told you before, I don't know where I came from or why I am here."

Astonishment at his abrupt reply rendered Alice speechless, and she glanced at Harry.

He raised his eyebrows and tilted his head slightly. "I see." Harry spoke slowly, as though trying to gain understanding while Alice didn't see at all.

"So, you don't remember where you lived as a child or what family you have?" Alice knew her voice was a higher pitch than usual, and she stopped and cleared her throat.

Ed slumped and shook his head miserably, like a homeless dog devoid of love.

Guilt, pity, and a desire to help surged through her. He had nobody except the community he served—who had all tried and failed to befriend him, including she and Harry.

"Well, it doesn't really matter who you are or what your history is. The main thing is you have a place to live and friends you can trust." Alice beamed at him and poured another cup of tea.

Ed shared the glimmer of a smile, and the air in the dining room seemed to clear.

Alice slathered butter on her bread and nibbled daintily at it while she tried to gather her thoughts. "You must have a look at our vegetable garden before you go. Perhaps you would like some seeds to add variety to your own?" She did her best to divert everyone's attention away from Ed's personal life. "Do you have a radio?"

"No. If I need to know, someone always tells me."

Harry laughed then and drained his cup. "Now *that* I can imagine."

Ed pushed his chair back and began to rise. "Thank you very much, Mrs Simpson. I go now. I will see your garden next time."

"You're very welcome, Ed. Thank you again for fixing the engine for us, and for everything else you do for this community. I believe the government are considering selling off land out this way, so it won't be long before we have more families move here and perhaps then, we will also get a mail service." She smiled at him and stood back as he ducked his head and lunged down the steps to the outside world.

Rock jumped to his feet and followed the men while Flossie slapped her tail on the floor and grimaced at Alice.

She bent and rubbed her ears. "So, what do you make of all that then? Do we have a new friend or was his visit a one-off? He said he would come again, so I suppose we'll just have to wait and see."

Flossie wagged her tail harder and rolled on her back.

"Anyway, what are you doing in here? The shearers arrive tomorrow, and you've got work to do."

Flossie ignored her, and Alice chuckled and went back inside.

CHAPTER 21

Two weeks passed before Alice had time to think about Christmas again. With heavy clouds building and three hundred sheep still to shear, Harry and the boys frantically mustered the animals, filling every pen inside the shed and under the raised floor with their heavily fleeced forms. While blustery showers swept across the land, the boys moved the dry sheep from under the building and up the ramp, refilling each catching pen at the call of "Sheepo".

To hasten the process, Alice ran back and forth to the woolshed, transporting scones, sandwiches, and billies full of hot tea. At the end of each day, washed and in clean clothes, the tired and hungry men filled the dining room and polished off a meal of roast meat and vegetables, followed with a pudding. It may have been more work for her, but by the time the shearers waved goodbye, Alice felt a warm glow of satisfaction.

The atmosphere in the shed, the smell of lanolin, the hiss and clank of the shearing engine, and the clatter of hooves on the slatted wooden floor were music to her ears. It didn't matter that the boot room dripped with coats and muddy boots for a day or two—she was a welcome and appreciated part of the team and loved every minute of it.

"Let's have a trip to town tomorrow to pick up last-minute items for Christmas." Harry's gaze swept around his family as they scraped their plates clean. Exhaustion was evident, and John's head nodded, jerking forward for a second time as he struggled to stay awake.

"I think that's a lovely idea, and we all deserve a day off. What do you say, boys?" Alice beamed.

The last of the dried fruit had gone into the previous night's steamed pudding, and with the new bakery opening in town, she looked forward to trying one of the neat, square loaves, saving herself both work and time.

"Yes," Timmy screeched with excitement. "Sam said the paper shop has a whole shelf of games and toys. Maybe we'll see what Santa might bring us for Christmas?"

George glanced from Harry to Alice and rolled his eyes. At twelve and almost a high school student, George clearly had doubts about Santa, and Alice glared at him. He grinned back at her, obviously aware of her silent threat, and nodded at his brothers.

"That would be great. I want to see the display the children in town did in the shop windows," George said.

"Right. Away to your baths now, and I'll be in to say goodnight shortly," Alice said. Harry stood, grimacing, and reached down to rub his calf.

Alice bit her lip. "Don't worry about clearing the plates. Sit and get that leg up for a while."

"It's alright, love. It's just complaining about the amount of running around it's had to do lately."

"Well, I suggest you listen to it while I clear the table."

George loitered and Alice gritted her teeth as he dawdled, seemingly ignoring her.

"George. Would you go and run the bath for John please? Now!"

Their eldest son wrenched the door open and disappeared. Alice chastised herself for snapping. Harry was right. They were all exhausted, and she looked forward to tomorrow.

———

MAUD'S LETTER BURNED IN HER POCKET AS THEY meandered along the main street of Helensville. After entering the Why Not tea room, Alice gave their order to the cheerful woman at the counter then joined her family at the table facing the road. Evidence of Christmas was everywhere—rivalled only by the buzz of conversation that consumed the community. War.

While in the grocer's shop less than an hour earlier, two women wearing worried expressions had been standing in front of the tinned goods, dithering over their choices. Alice couldn't help but overhear their conversation about whether it would be prudent to stock up.

Having extra many mouths to feed was topmost in many minds.

Alice had shot the women a sympathetic smile. "I'll leave you to help these customers and come back later, Mr Jones. My order is on the counter, and we'll pick it up this afternoon. Thank you."

She looked across the table to Harry. "Everyone's worried at the moment. We don't know what will happen."

Harry nodded as George looked at them both solemnly. "But why are people worried? We live on the other side of the world to the trouble."

"I know it must be hard to understand, son." Harry drew a deep breath. "For many, the previous war is still etched in their memories, and the fear of the unknown makes things worse. We'll do everything we can to support our nation and our allies—and the best thing you boys can do for us all is to continue with your studies and be thankful that we don't live in Europe."

"Isn't the Christmas tree pretty?" John was staring dreamily at the pine tree out on the footpath.

Decorated with baubles and paper chains made from coloured paper, it was a welcome distraction, and as food was delivered to their table, Alice returned her attention to their upcoming celebrations. "When we get home, we'll sort out decorations and start getting ready for your cousins to arrive." Then she poured the tea, took a sandwich from the plate, and pulled Maud's letter from her pocket.

Innisfree

Kingseat

16 December 1939

Dear Alice,

I can't wait until we come up next week. Shearing will be over for you by now, and our milkman seems to have settled in (and doing a good job, thank goodness!). We are preparing for our little holiday.

The children will bring their bathing suits and are hoping that Harry will take them fishing? Two days is not long, and I'm quite sure the preparation is more time-consuming and stressful than the journey—but you and I both know it will be worth every minute of it.

Dougal's sending two horses on the train, so we will be leaving him in Helensville, and I will drive the car to your place. I'm terrified, but if you can do it so often, surely I can manage once (I am so impressed with your driving ability). At least I know I don't have to turn off anywhere, so I shouldn't get lost. Dougal will be an hour or two behind me, riding one horse and leading the other.

Did you receive a letter from Lily? She gave birth to her fourth child (another boy!) in November. Isn't she amazing? In her forties and has had a baby almost every year since marrying! If mother was alive, I'm sure she would be thrilled (or perhaps sympathetic?).

Eve and Mary came for afternoon tea last week and, of course, are full of gossip. They didn't like my suggestion of them doing more for the community. Eve's children are now old enough for her to return to teaching—or at least help out at the local school, and Mary knits so beautifully I suggested she begin making warm socks to send with the young men in our district who have volunteered. I don't do nearly as much as you do on the farm, but at least you and I never acquired the airs and graces of our older sisters. I suppose it's one of the few advantages of us being so young when mother passed on.

Anyway, I had better get back into the kitchen. I'll bring plenty of food to share, so we certainly won't starve.

Looking forward to seeing you all soon.

Lots of love,

Maud

Alice raised her eyes as Timmy swiped the last sandwich from the plate.

"Much news?" Harry asked.

"Not really. They're all looking forward to their holiday, and the boys want you to take them fishing. Oh, and Dougal is sending two horses on the train.

He'll collect them from the railhead and ride them home for us."

"Wonderful. So does that mean Maud will drive?" He grinned.

"Yes, she will. And I'm sure she will do a fine job of it," Alice replied tartly. "Now, if everyone's finished, I suggest we collect our supplies and make our way home. I want Paddy to help me in the garden, so it looks its best before they arrive." She swept up her bag and tucked her hand into the crook of Harry's arm. He smiled, put his hat on, and they led the boys out onto the footpath.

———

"THEY'RE COMING!" ALICE PEERED OUT THE WINDOW AS Timmy yelled from his perch high up in the puriri tree before scrambling to the ground and running across the lawn. John followed close behind, his descent slow due to him straddling a low branch, pretending it was a racehorse.

The big grey car thrummed and rattled as it climbed the hill and pulled to a halt in the yard, directly in front of the freshly painted sign that read *Fantail Ridge*. It was three o'clock in the afternoon of Christmas Eve.

Alice had untied her apron, straightened the hydrangeas in the jug on the front hall stand, and hurried down the steps outside. As Maud stepped out of the car, Alice threw her arms around her exhilarated sister.

"We made it. I mean, I drove all the way from Helensville, and we got here safely."

Alice laughed and bent to hug Catherine. Ken met her eye to eye before hugging her and stepped back to let Hamish take his turn.

"You boys have got so tall."

"I'm gasping for a cup of tea," Maud said. "Actually, having just negotiated that road, I believe I could even handle something stronger."

Alice raised her eyebrows and grinned. "I'll make you tea. You can have a wee dram of whisky with that husband of yours later if your nerves are still frazzled."

Maud laughed and turned to the rear of the vehicle where the older boys were dragging out suitcases and boxes.

"Be careful with that one." She pointed to a wooden crate filled with tins packed between tea towels and old bleached flour bags. "That's a sponge cake and a double batch of shortbread—which I hope is not in a million pieces after its journey."

George nodded and placed it carefully on the ground before he lifted out a box of plums.

"This is all the orchard had. Mrs Grzesiek said the apricots won't be long, but you'll have to wait until February for the peaches and nectarines."

"Thanks, Maudie. They'll be lovely. I'll stew some up and make a sponge topping for pudding tonight.

Everyone can help themselves to them while they're fresh. Come on now. Let's get the kettle on and put your luggage away."

The only other time Maud and her family had visited was before the house was built, and they'd pitched a big square canvas tent on the front lawn for extra accommodation. Now Alice proudly showed her through the house, delighted that the carpet runner had finally been delivered and the new lino in the bathroom shone.

"I thought the four older boys might like to sleep out in the shearer's room, and John and Catherine can have the boys' room." She led the way to the end of the hallway where a door opened onto a small porch overlooking the lawn, puriri tree, and Alice's park beyond. On either side of the hall were two bedrooms. "This is yours." Alice waved her arm, indicating for Maud to enter first.

"It's beautiful." Maud's gaze swept from the double bed covered with a woven cotton spread, up the walls, and onto the ceiling which she studied for so long, Alice fidgeted nervously. "I love the ceiling. Are they the same throughout the house?"

"Yes. All the same, and I agree—I love them. Apparently, that's the latest style, according to the plasterer."

Made of textured plaster, the bedroom ceiling was divided into four large squares and supported by deep timber boards. Pale wallpaper covered with tiny pink flowers decorated the top half of the walls while the lower half were lined with dark stained wood to match the doors and trims.

"Come and see our room."

Maud followed Alice across the hall and into the larger bedroom. Similar to the guest room, the main bedroom also had built-in wardrobes, a matching chest of drawers, cupboard, and dressing table. The exception was the beautiful, engraved bed. Soft avocado floral wallpaper was accented by striped olive green and white curtains hanging on either side of the window.

"Very nice. It seems so big compared to your little house in Karaka."

"It is—and hopefully all we'll ever want or need. I must admit, I feel a bit like royalty but, having lived in the shed for so long, am relishing every minute."

"Mum, Uncle Dougal's here!" George hollered down the hallway, and the sisters hurried outside.

Harry, Paddy, and the children were clustered in front of two horses, with Dougal standing dwarf-like between them. One was a magnificent Clydesdale, his glossy coat a deep mushroom colour with a salt and pepper tail, his white mane and legs dusted brown from the dirt road. The other horse was slightly smaller with a mottled grey coat and a long, thick mane and tail.

"This big fellow is called Major." Dougal handed the Clydesdale's reins to Harry and turned to the grey horse. "And this kind gentleman is Bobby. He's not exactly in his youth but has been a wonderful hunter for my friend, Ritchie."

"So why didn't he want to keep him?" Alice asked.

"The horse has been idling in a paddock ever since Ritchie had a stroke, and when I asked if he wanted to sell him, he refused to begin with. I mentioned why I wanted him, and he must have given it more thought because he caught up with me a week later and said he'd never sell but would be happy to let him come and live here—free of charge as long as he was loved."

John stood under the horse's nose and reached up, touching him lightly on the muzzle. As though reading the child's mind, the horse lowered his head and blew softly, ruffling John's hair, then remained perfectly still while Catherine joined her cousin and stroked him gently.

"He'll be a great horse for the children—or any of you, for that matter. Used to harness, too, so you could put him in traces if you want to. Major is one of ours, and he's reliable enough for farm work. He's a bit quieter than a couple of the others I've got but not so keen to cooperate in a team, which is what I need. So … what do you think?" Dougal finished his speech, his gaze alternating between Harry and Alice.

"I can't thank you enough. Both look perfect," Harry said.

"The first thing you'll need to do is to make a step ladder for us all." Alice laughed as excitement bubbled. She loved these gentle giants and was elated at the prospect of being able to let Duke ease back from the heavy work. She beamed at the men and took a deep breath.

"Come on then. You put the horses away, and I'll concentrate on refreshments. I think it's time for a cold drink and a piece of Christmas cake before we do the evening chores." She grinned at the hopeful look on Dougal's face. "Yes, Dougal, there's a whisky waiting for you too."

CHAPTER 22

As though wanting to tempt their guests, the weather over the peninsula remained perfect for the whole Christmas period. Pohutukawa flowers glowed red, smothering the trees more prolifically than ever, the wind blew a gentle, cooling breeze, and the sun hovered above, sending down just enough heat to make outdoor life pleasant without burning everyone to a crisp.

George's attempt at preparing a goose for the table was a great success, and accompanied by freshly dug potatoes, peas, and a range of roast vegetables from both Maud and Alice's gardens, the crowd in the dining room declared they would have to put dessert off for an hour before they could fit it in.

When the pudding was finally eaten, and disappointment at not finding a threepenny piece in their serving was overcome, the children trooped outside to play with the new cricket set and climb the puriri tree.

It was almost four o'clock before the lethargic adults galvanised themselves into action and declared the beach was beckoning. While the children pulled on swimsuits and packed dilly bags with towels and dry clothes, the men disappeared outside to prepare the truck, and Maud and Alice filled the picnic basket.

Water sparkled in the late sunshine while gentle waves lapped the shoreline, leaving a narrow strip of sand against the grassed track. Toetoe was in full bloom, and tuis hovered around the flax flowers, drinking their nectar, and warily watching the intruders.

"Off you go then. Not too deep, remember?" Maud spoke sternly, and John frowned at her before turning to Alice.

"Come with me, Mum?" His voice was tight with worry as his brothers and cousins leapt and splashed, waist-deep in water.

"I'll just come in a little way. You're alright. Flossie will look after you. Won't you, girl." Alice hitched up her dress and tied the skirt in a loose knot above her knees. She walked next to her son as they picked their way through the shallow waves with John clasping Flossie's collar firmly.

Alice didn't own a swimsuit and turned to Maud.

"Are you coming in?"

"Absolutely not. I'm quite comfortable here, thank

you very much." And she plonked herself on the rug spread across the sand.

Harry and Paddy unravelled the mullet net and with Dougal's help, made their way into the water and, waist-deep, swept a large semi-circle before returning to the shore. A number of mullet flapped, trapped within the confines of their webbed prison, while the children splashed and shrieked with excitement.

"I think this might be your solitary giant approaching?" Maud whispered as she sidled up to Alice at the water's edge.

Alice glanced along the beach and waved. "It is," she hissed. Raising her voice, she called out to him. "Hello, Ed. Would you like to join us? We're just about to have our picnic."

The big man stared, expressionless for a few seconds before shaking his head. "Thank you but no. I have scallops to bag before the boat comes tonight."

"Ooh, how nice. I love scallops," Maud said, and nudged Alice subtly with her elbow.

"Ed, this is my sister Maud."

He gave her a small bow as though considering Maud some form of monarch.

Alice rolled her eyes and waved her arm towards the men. "The man in the straw hat is Dougal, Maud's husband. And the extra three children in the water belong to them." Alice smiled as she stepped gently on Maud's foot in an attempt to prevent her from cross-questioning Ed. Maud took the hint and stood still, her expression polite and … regal?

As Ed doffed his hat and continued to his dingy, Alice pulled her sister onto the rug and shook her head. "You're such a busybody," she hissed. They looked at each other and chuckled.

"I know. But don't you wanted to know his story? Why does he live here all on his own with nothing to do except fish … Well, and grow his vegetables and exchange freight and groceries with the boats as they pass?"

"Of course I'd love to know. But he's so private. It's taken four years to get him to have a cup of tea with us. If you'd given him your usual inquisition, he would probably run a mile and we'd be back to square one again."

"Hmm. You have to admit though, he's the most interesting person we've met in a long while. Where's he from? He doesn't say much, but when he does, his voice has something. I don't know what, but it's like he doesn't know what words to use and has to think about every one before he speaks."

Alice didn't answer as the children arrived, dripping and flicking sand onto the rug.

"I'm starving," Timmy said.

"Well, before we eat, you need to get dried and dressed. There's plenty of privacy behind the truck if you need it, Catherine." Alice got to her feet. "I'll come with you."

By the time they returned, Maud had set out the plate of cold goose and leftover potatoes and was slicing the bread, fresh from the morning's oven.

In spite of everyone having consumed the generous midday meal, the food disappeared within minutes, washed down with the flagon of homemade lemonade saved especially for Christmas.

As the tide began to recede, Harry built a fire on the edge of the damp sand and, huddled on towels and sacks from the back of the truck, they sat around the flickering flames and waited for the billy to boil.

Soon after sunset, they piled back into the truck and made their way home, hurried through the bath, and gathered around the piano in the small sitting room. Alice began playing 'Away in a Manger', and the children sang at the top of their voices, as though trying to outdo one another.

After a dozen more Christmas carols, Catherine made a request. "Can we sing *All things Bright and Beautiful* please, Aunty Alice?"

"Of course. This is the last one though as it's bedtime for you all." It had been her favourite hymn for as long as she could remember, and she closed her eyes and thought of Emmie as her fingers caressed the keys.

Weariness had filtered into the close-knit band of children and parents. Their voices softened, and as the final words echoed around the room, a peace settled over Alice—one she had not felt since before her daughter died. Her fingers trailed over the keyboard and lay silently for a few seconds before she closed the lid and turned to face the singers. "Thank you all for a wonderful Christmas." Her voice was barely more than a whisper, and she swallowed hard.

Maud put her arm around her shoulders, and the sisters clung together for a moment in silence.

"Right then. Time for bed, everyone. Tomorrow is another big day." Maud clapped her hands together as she spoke.

There was not one complaint as the tired children kissed their parents goodnight and trooped out of the room. For Alice, Christmas of 1939 was unforgettable.

———

IN THE EARLY MORNING, WHEN THE SUN'S RAYS HAD barely covered the lawn, Alice and Maud set off for a walk. With no sound from the children's rooms, Alice had whispered in Harry's ear, "We'll be back within the hour."

He'd murmured incoherently and she tiptoed out of the room.

The two women negotiated the steep decline behind the cow paddock and joined the track that wound through the bush. Fantails greeted them with a friendly wiggle of their tails and their high-pitched chatter.

"Isn't it cool and pretty?" Maud gazed around her and her shoulders lowered.

"It's my favourite place. Not that I get much time to come here, but nevertheless, I always feel rejuvenated after a walk along this track." Alice held out her hand and brushed the ferns gently as they passed. Droplets flicked off the fronds and onto the carpet of leaves underfoot. "When John first started school, I often walked this way down to the flat and met the boys coming home. Don't do it much now though, because apparently having your mother meet you after school is not really welcomed once they consider themselves old hands."

They both giggled and ducked under the punga tree as the track opened onto the flat paddock.

"Now we have to go back up again, so take a big breath and put your best foot forward," Alice said.

Neither of them spoke as they toiled up the steep roadside. The banks on the top side of the hill shone as tiny rivulets of water dripped down the deep golden face. While on the lower edge, the road dropped away to reveal Alice's emerging parkland, dotted with steadily growing trees, waving buttercups, and dandelions.

On reaching the top, they rested on the wooden bench beneath the puriri tree and caught their breaths. Alice clasped Maud's pale, soft fingers in hers, and they sat in contented silence for a long moment before getting to their feet and dawdling inside.

———

IT WAS LATE MORNING BEFORE MAUD AND DOUGAL packed the car and said their goodbyes. A basket of leftover food was nestled between them on the front seat, waiting until they reached the other side of Helensville before it would be opened.

Following the bustle of the usual chores and the emotions of farewell, Alice paused her kneading of bread dough and stared out of the kitchen window, her gaze resting on the fuchsia bush with its pink and purple flowers shaped like tiny ballerinas. It would be months or even longer before she and Maud would see one another again, and an emptiness deep inside her gnawed. Self-pity and a sliver of loneliness crept through her. She looked down at the dough and resumed kneading, forcing her thoughts to other things—things that must be faced.

A World War was raging, and New Zealand naval ships had been deployed to Europe. Men around the country were volunteering in droves while branches of the Home Guard were formed in towns and cities. The fact that both Dougal and Harry would be part of the home-based organisation and not sent overseas should have been a solace to Alice. Instead, she worried that they might be considered pacifists or conscientious objectors.

Kenneth and George were moving onto high school, and it came as a shock to her that life as they knew it may never be the same again.

She took a deep breath and shook her head in an

effort to rid herself of negative thoughts. The tin on the shed roof opposite the house crackled as the sun beat more intensely, and she turned her thoughts to the next big event on the farm—haymaking.

This year, four of their biggest fields had been shut up for hay, and with the early summer rain and a run of hot days predicted to turn into weeks, it was time to cut the first paddock.

Alice forced a smile, immediately feeling brighter. Haymaking was always busy even if fraught with angst when clouds formed overhead. However, it was also one of her favourite times of the year. The boys loved working alongside the team of men that banded together to help one another—particularly when rain threatened. With talk of petrol rationing running rampant in the community, it was possible that for the foreseeable future the horses may prove more of an advantage than the recently purchased Farmall tractor —Harry's pride and joy.

Alice gave the dough a final slap, pushed it into the tin, and set it to the side of the stove to prove. Then, reaching for her hat, she marched out the back door and across the yard.

"Hi, Mum, we're greasing the hay mower," Timmy said.

Harry looked up and grinned at Alice. All four of them were covered in dirt and spiders webs. However, Timmy was a clear winner with grease on his face, hands, and down the front of his overalls. He wore a smile that spread from ear to ear.

"I'm the mechanic," he announced.

"And I'm the horse man," John added.

Alice glanced at George, and her face softened. He was going through a growth spurt. Trouser hems sat above his ankle bones, while thin arms appeared more gangly than usual under the rolled-up sleeves. Her son would be a man in no time. Meanwhile, he seemed content to follow his father's instructions and continue through life in his own serious and studious manner. For this, and so much more, Alice was thankful.

CHAPTER 23

Innisfree
Kingseat
24 April 1941

Dear Alice,

Can you believe that winter is nearly here already? Did you get your spring bulbs planted before the rain started? I didn't bother this year—hopefully it won't make much difference. Vegetables are more important. Dougal had planned to plant oats and was devastated to discover the rats had got into his grain store. He'll plant what's left and hope that we get a crop of some sort. Life on the land certainly is full of highs and lows!

We heard on the radio this morning that things are happening quickly for our overseas troops. New Zealand's 2nd Division (the one stationed in Egypt) are being deployed to take part in the defence of Greece. We're not certain but think that it's the troop our neighbour's son is part of. She will be worried sick, but nothing we can do from here. I'll take a cake over to her tomorrow and have a chat. They keep bees, and with the sugar rations, I'm finding honey very useful for baking—she usually gives me a jar to bring home and I use it wisely.

I believe we'll be experiencing a lot more rationing before too long due to imports and exports being hampered. Our poor friends and family in Britain are struggling, and a large portion of our foodstuffs are being supplied to the American forces in the South Pacific now. We're so lucky we can grow our own and not be hungry. For once, I'm pleased we have a dairy farm, especially now our milker has been called up. The negative of that is that we have to milk the whole herd on our own every day.

On another note, you should see the Epsom show grounds. It's now a military base and apparently will remain so until the end of the war. Catherine and I had a day in the city over the Easter break, and it was very strange to stop off in Greenlane (we walked up to Cornwall Park where we met Frank for a half-hour brother-sister catch up). There was no sign of the Ferris wheel or anything resembling our normal agricultural show. I bought a piece of grey fabric to make a skirt for each of us and also trousers for the boys at Milne and Choyce. They're getting tall, and finding suitable clothing and fabric is getting hard and is so expensive. I must admit, the city had a different atmosphere to normal, and we were both very glad to get home again.

The local children have been told they have to find other

options for travel to and from school in case of bombing. I felt quite sick when they came home and told me that, however it seems they just have to know a cross-country path that avoids the main roads. I don't suppose you have to worry about that sort of thing.

Dougal has been going to the weekly Home Guard meetings and seems to be quite enjoying it—even if it's not intended to be a social get together. Our Women's Division still meet once a month, and although we mostly discuss ways of supporting the war effort, it's nice to dress up a bit and be social.

Both Eve and Mary took heed of my comments soon after the war began and are now involved in various voluntary groups. As you can imagine, Eve is already president of one of them! I don't see them (E and M) as often as we only go to church once a month and have cancelled our family lunches —everyone is too busy or doesn't want to use up their precious petrol ration by attending. I feel guilty admitting it, but a fortnightly letter to and from each of them seems sufficient in these awful times.

Well, I suppose I should finish now as the rain has stopped, and there is always plenty to do outside. Sorry if this letter seems to be a bit morbid—a sign of the times.

Thinking of you as always and looking forward to your news.

Love to you all,
Maud

Alice put the letter down and glanced out the window. It was raining again, but not the heavy downpours of the previous few days. This time, the showers had lightened, and a vibrant rainbow arched over the harbour. With the boys at school, and both Harry and Paddy catching up with maintenance in the machinery shed, she picked up her writing pad, pausing for a moment. The pen hovered over the page, and she chewed her lip. There was so much to say and yet there was nothing. Each day followed a similar routine to the previous, each chore was the same as before, and now everyone was extra busy with their various activities and efforts to make life as normal as possible.

She sighed and began.

Fantail Ridge
South Head
1 May 1941

Dear Maud,

I have just received your letter and decided to respond immediately while I have no other distractions. (I'm sure you know what I mean!).

Like you, we are doing our best to keep our spirits up and to try to live as normally as possible. I am missing my trips to town—we have reduced our shopping to once every six weeks at most and work in with others in the community to deliver and pick up various things when we go.

I've also decided to give my ration books to the grocer. There are many people in town who are worse off than us, and other than flour, sugar, and tea, we really don't need anything. Our veggie garden and fruit trees provide us well and having two house cows now means I have more than enough milk and cream—so much so that we are feeding the excess milk and veggies to two young pigs that we got from a neighbour. They are growing well (the pigs, that is, not the neighbour!) and will be the perfect size to provide pork and bacon for us by late winter. We haven't had mutton for a while but are still catching fish regularly, and between Harry, Vince, and Clive, we manage to share a venison every now and again. With the odd wild pig and the start of duck shooting season now here, we won't be hungry!

The Home Guard did an exercise on our neighbour's place last week (Charlie's property—up the road towards the Tasman). Unlike Dougal's troupe, they only get together once a month because of the isolation. They conduct a few night exercises—plus of course their two-week camp each year. Our local school headmaster, Maurice, is involved and is apparently very good with radio communications. On the exercise at Charlie's, they had to set up radio contact with Helensville from the highest sand blow on his land. Poor Maurice was the only one not able to ride a horse, so he said he'd participate on foot. Evidently, he didn't realise how heavy the radio and battery would be to carry and had a devil of a job making the rendezvous on time. He was scratched and battered from crashing through the tea tree and lupin and was totally exhausted by the time he got there. I admire him for his courage and dedication. What's more— he's a great teacher!

Like your children, ours were also told they had to find a route home that didn't involve the roads. A bit easier here as they just go across the paddocks. Easy for ours, I mean, but not so good for the poor little ones who live miles farther out. Still, if the bus couldn't run, everyone would pitch in, so it's not really a problem.

Thanks for the updates on our sisters. I haven't had a letter for a while now, although I wrote to them both a couple of weeks ago.

I can hear Harry and Paddy outside—lunchtime already! The days fly.

Thinking of you too—as always.

Much love to you and yours,

Alice

"I LOVE THE SCHOOL HOLIDAYS," TIMMY ANNOUNCED.

He and John were bouncing around in the back seat while Alice drove, and she was not quite sure whether they were more excited about their trip to town or meeting George off the train.

Alice greeted her gangly teenager with a kiss on the cheek. He shrugged away, and she smiled in her attempt to hide her surprise.

Once back at the car and away from fellow students, he threw his arms around her in a bear hug, and she gave a sigh of relief. "Sorry, dear, I didn't mean to embarrass you at the station. We're very pleased to have you home. How's boarding school?"

George shrugged and said nothing. By the time they had collected supplies and the post, he was back to his old self. Stripped of his tie and blazer, he teased his brothers in the back of the car, and Alice was relieved when they reached the final hill before home.

"I want to catch Bobby and ride over the farm—to blow a few cobwebs away," George said. They had barely walked through the door, and Alice was dying for a cup of tea.

"I want to come too," John said.

"Why don't we all go for a ride? We can shift that mob of cattle while we're at it," Harry said.

Alice sighed and acquiesced. It seemed an age since they had all been out on the farm together and, in the last golden days of autumn, they couldn't have picked a nicer day.

Harry and George headed off to catch the horses, while Alice hurriedly changed into her trousers and warm jersey before checking the casserole in the oven.

Stormy whinnied and hobbled up and down the fence as they rode away, his age and arthritis now affecting his ability to be ridden. Alice had suggested they pass him on to the Bennetts for their youngest children but had received protests from the boys.

"He's worked hard all his life, and he needs us to look after him now," George said.

John and Timmy had seconded George's statement, and in the end, they all agreed.

"At least he's got company here, and when other

children come to visit who don't ride much, he can be used," Harry said.

Timmy led the entourage on Duke, closely followed by George and John, double-dinking on Bobby's broad back. Alice kicked Blaze into a trot to ride alongside Harry. Appearing small on Major, her husband smiled at her as the big horse clumped along on massive hooves, partially disguised under their skirt of white hair. Trailing the band of riders, Rock and Flossie trotted briskly, their tails held high and drooling with apparent anticipation.

They dropped into single file to dip into the gully and rose to the crest of the hill on the other side. As the track opened up again, George leaned forward with John's arms wrapped tightly around his waist, kicked Bobby into a canter, and let out a whoop.

Not to be outdone, Timmy urged Duke into his ungainly swinging trot, and Alice turned to Harry. "Are you ready?"

"You're on."

Alice shortened her reins and stood lightly in her stirrups as Blaze bounded into a gallop. Her headscarf was knotted tightly, and the corners flapped against her neck while her eyes watered, the wind whipping her face. They covered the length of the paddock in a matter of seconds, drawing to a halt at the gate, behind which a herd of Hereford cattle raised big white faces and stared at the new arrivals. Their deep brown coats glistening in the sunlight, some turned around and hesitated, seemingly undecided about whether they should run or not.

"C'mon, c'mon!" Harry's voice deepened as he bent to unlatch the gate. The cattle took a step or two forward then stopped hesitantly.

In silence, Alice and the boys trooped into the paddock, filing past Harry and waiting while he closed the gate. Still puffing from her exhilarating gallop, Alice raised a hand to her burning cheeks.

By the time she caught her breath, the boys had veered away, spreading out in a semi-circle behind the cattle, together with the dogs. Leading the herd at a steady walk, Harry rode to the paddock beyond them and once again opened the gate and moved to the side. In a rush, the mob trotted through the opening and quickly dropped their heads, fanning out in the knee-deep grass.

"Thanks, troops. Another job done." Harry grinned and gazed towards the east. Across the other side of the harbour, the hills darkened, and the water rippled, shimmering under the rapidly setting sun.

The breeze was gentle but cold, and the riders turned for home.

CHAPTER 24

It was late that night before Alice remembered the pile of mail she had plonked on the desk in the corner of the living room. The boys had sat up playing cards and talking until John eventually gave in and, yawning, led the withdrawal to the bedroom.

Flicking through the pile of newspapers and letters, Alice paused, frowning as she held up a small, white envelope.

"This is addressed to you, Harry." She turned it over and peered at the tiny, scrawled writing. In blotched black ink, it looked more like a spider had crawled across the paper after first walking through paint. "It's from someone called R. Davidson."

Harry shot her a blank stare and shrugged. "Let me see." He reached out to take the envelope.

Studying the writing, he shook his head slowly and picked up the letter knife. He sliced the envelope open and withdrew the sheaf of thin papers. A second piece of paper fell to the floor, folded into quarters, its parchment yellowed, and its corners tattered.

"Do you know anyone called Davidson?" Alice asked.

"No." Harry unfolded the letter and read for a minute before looking up at Alice with surprise. "It's about a young fellow I used to know—Roy Meiklejohn. The letter is from his sister."

"Why would she be writing to you?"

His frown deepened, and he slumped into the armchair. "He was in my troop in Egypt. A nice lad. One of those uncoordinated young men who never quite seemed to get the hang of marching. He kind of waddled—you know, where the left arm and leg went at the same time instead of alternately like everyone else."

She nodded and perched on the sofa opposite him. "Go on then, read it out."

Waipiro

East Cape

10 May 1941

Dear Mr Simpson,

I write this with sincere apologies and hope you will understand. First, please let me introduce myself.

My name is Ruth Davidson, sister of Roy Meiklejohn, who I believe you befriended during WW1 when you both served in the Mounted Troops in Egypt. I understand you lost contact when he was injured and sent to England to recover. He was eventually shipped home and spoke frequently and kindly of you. Sadly, Roy never fully recovered from his war injuries, although he was a comfort to our mother, with whom he lived.

In October 1935, Roy drowned in a boating accident, and our mother moved in with my husband and I until her recent death. While sorting through her possessions, I found the enclosed letter, which you will see is addressed to yourself as simply Harry Simpson, Karaka. I read the letter, which, for unknown reasons, Mother kept instead of posting.

He may have mentioned a mare he had, his favourite, who he called Lorna and from whom he bred a beautiful foal after his return to us in 1918. Initially, Roy was able to continue riding, and his horses were his one and only true love. After Lorna died from old age, her foal (Beauty) became his pride and joy as there was nothing she wouldn't or couldn't do for him. Eventually, when she was around ten years old, he put her to a stallion belonging to a friend over near Gisborne way, and the result was a very nice bay colt with a thick blaze down his nose. Roy rode the young horse everywhere once old enough and named him "The Brigadier". Unfortunately, Roy's injury plagued him, and in early 1935, he was so crippled he was unable to ride anymore.

We will never know if his drowning was accidental or otherwise as he was alone when he advised he was going fishing. However, the enclosed letter was apparently left inside a box he kept labelled "important rubbish". Mother was distraught following his death, and we left much of the arrangements for his funeral and belongings to be dealt with by a good friend and neighbour. I am not aware of conversa-tions that may have taken place regarding the horses, but the neighbour advised that Roy always said, should anything happen to him, he (our neighbour) was to take care of Beauty and The Brigadier was to be sent to a friend he had got to know in the war. I can only presume that you were the friend to whom he referred and that Roy divulged your name to him.

I don't know if you ever received the horse or what may have happened to him if you didn't? If, by some chance, you took receipt of him, I would be grateful if you would advise accordingly.

We may have gone through our lives having no idea of your existence except for a chance encounter recently with a visitor, who spoke of selling sheep to someone of your name who had relocated from Karaka to South Head, via Helensville.

The enclosed letter, written in 1935 by Roy, had not been thrown out, and your name jogged my memory. I retrieved it and hope and pray that it is the final piece in what appears to have been quite a puzzle?

I look forward to your reply.

Yours sincerely,

Ruth Davidson (nee Meiklejohn)

"Oh my goodness—Blaze." Alice put her palms against her cheeks as her eyes met Harry's.

"I'll say. Poor Roy. What a kind gesture though. And why me? I would have thought he'd have plenty of other people to give a horse to?"

"Read what he says. Perhaps that will explain more." Alice pointed to the single sheet that had fallen to the floor. She picked it up and passed it to him, waiting impatiently while he carefully prised the folds open and hesitatingly began to read.

October 1935

To my friend, Harry Simpson, Karaka, South Auckland,

Sorry I have not tried to contact you since the war. I have never forgotten the help you gave me when my horse died in Egypt. Your kindness and support in helping me bury him and then finding me another was more than anyone has ever shown, and I regret that I was never able to thank you properly. My health has not been good since the war, and I am no longer able to ride, which disturbs me greatly. Please give The Brigadier a good home. I know he will serve you well.

Sincerely,

Roy Meiklejohn

Alice blinked back a tear, her eyes glued to Harry's bowed head.

He sat in silence for a full minute before he took a deep breath and faced her. "It sounds as though perhaps his drowning was not an accident." Harry spoke slowly, a sadness in his voice that melted Alice's heart. She moved to squeeze into the chair next to him, wrapping her arms around his shoulders, pressing her cheek against his.

They remained still and silent until, eventually, Harry sighed, refolded the letters. and carefully slid them back in the envelope. "Well, that's the mystery solved, anyway. Our Blaze is really Roy's Brigadier."

"We won't change his name though, will we?"

"No. We've had him for nearly six years, so I'm sure he won't mind." Harry moved as if to stand, and Alice slid off the chair.

"Tomorrow we will both write to Ruth and thank her," she said. "But now, I think it's time for bed."

Alice lay awake for what seemed like hours, thinking about how much she had to tell Maud in her next letter. Finally, Harry's rhythmic breaths brushed against her hair. She drew the eiderdown up around her neck, closed her eyes, and succumbed to a dreamless sleep.

CHAPTER 25

Winter of 1941 was cold, finishing with the wettest August Alice could remember. For weeks on end the rain slashed at the windows and soaked into every crevice, ditch, and stream. Springs burst out of the banks and hills and surged into valleys, overflowing drains, and eventually spilling into the harbour. Even the animals seemed sick of the rain as they hung around under trees, heads bowed, or huddled together against the hay sheds and heavy timber gates. Mud threatened to reach the top of everyone's gumboots, and the racks of wet washing hanging around and above the fire annoyed Alice, hampering her efforts to cook for the family.

It had been two months since anyone had been to town, and she peered into the flour bin anxiously. There was just enough for two loaves of bread and no more. She screwed up her nose and sighed. To make matters worse, the telephone line must have come down somewhere as there had been no service for days, if not weeks. Apart from Harry, Paddy, and the boys, she had seen no one since the community church service, held in the school six weeks before.

Deciding there was no option, she donned her thickest skirt and long wool socks and covered them with a heavy oilskin coat. Tying a sou'wester hat under her chin, she slipped the strap of a leather satchel over her head and tucked it under her coat.

"I'm walking down to the wharf to see what stores I can get from Ed." Alice had to raise her voice over the noise as Harry and Paddy hammered loudly in competition with the rain. The forge was red hot in the shed, and both men wore thick gloves and held shields in front of their faces. Harry lay the set of hames he was holding against the wall and moved over to Alice.

"We're making a new set so we can use the plough and the sled at the same time," he shouted.

Alice nodded. Until a month ago, they'd only had one full set of harness, so they'd had to use each horse until they became tired, then switch the gear over and continue. It was both slow and inefficient, so both men had been cutting and stitching leather for days. It appeared they were now ready to shape the steel parts that would run along the horses' sides and link with whichever vehicle or piece of equipment they would pull.

"I'm almost out of flour, so I'm going to see if I can get some from Ed." Alice leaned into Harry as she spoke.

"Good luck. Have you got your waders on?" Harry grinned and gave her a peck on the cheek.

She waved and turned away, bent her head, and plodded steadily along the road and down the hill towards the wharf. For once, Flossie didn't follow her, choosing instead to stay in the back room with Rock where the warm air from the fridge's motor floated out the vent and over the dog's favourite resting spot.

"Are you there, Ed?" Alice called loudly as she approached the shack. As usual, there was little sign of life, with the exception of a few bedraggled seagulls strolling up and down the wharf, pecking at invisible specks in the timber.

The big man loomed suddenly in the doorway, and Alice started. He stooped a little and peered into her face. "Oh, Mrs Simpson. It's you."

Alice shot him a wry grin. "Not exactly my going-to-town outfit, but yes. It's me under these oilskins."

He nodded and stood silently, as though waiting for her to explain her presence.

"I need some flour, Ed. Do you have any in the store?" She crossed her fingers under the overlong sleeves of the coat.

Although referred to as "the store", the wharf and shack were now little more than a facility for the peninsula's residents to have goods delivered to or picked up from by the boats that plied the harbour. In earlier days, it had held an odd variety of essentials, but with every improvement to the road and with more families moving into the district, Ed's services were fast becoming redundant. As his supplies dwindled, he became more reclusive than ever.

He shook his head, and his face took on an expression not unlike that of a bloodhound.

Alice's hopes plummeted. "Are the boats still able to call in?"

"Once or twice a week, when tide permits."

"Of course, when tide permits," she repeated under her breath.

Since war had been declared, every vessel and vehicle requiring fuel had been reassessed and restricted by rationing. A surge of annoyance ran briefly through Alice. There was little convenience at the best of times, but now, even the word seemed superfluous.

"I have some flour in my hut. Enough to share. Come."

Alice's face lit up at Ed's words, and she willingly followed him inside.

After lifting the calico bag onto the table, he stretched his long arm out to collect a tin from the shelf. Then he proceeded to transfer flour from the bag, one cup at a time, until the tin was full. He handed the cloth bag, complete with two thirds of its original contents, to Alice. She had expected him to pass her the tin containing the smaller quantity and was taken aback by his generosity.

"I will order more when the next boat comes."

"Oh thank you very much." She hesitated for a few seconds, and then blurted, "Would you like to join us for tea on Sunday night? It's a long time since we've had anyone visit, and I would like to thank you for this." She pointed to the bag and tilted her head to one side as she waited.

On the opposite side of the table, his tall, rigid stance was imposing as he stared at her. In the silence, Alice was sure he would hear her heart thumping, in spite of the rain outside.

"Thank you. I will."

Fully expecting a rebuff, Alice's jaw dropped. "G-great. See you after five o'clock on Sunday evening then."

She knew better than to offer to collect him. With the exception of a sled that he dragged behind him, and the dingy he kept tied to the wharf, no one had ever seen him use a vehicle of any kind or accept a lift with anybody. She shoved the bag of flour into her satchel and buttoned the coat over it.

Giving a small smile and a wave, she turned and made her way back along the muddy track. As she reached the road, she glanced towards the grey timber wharf, barely visible amongst the flax and grasses growing along the water's edge. There was no sign of him. No sign of life, not even the seagulls.

She strode up the hill towards home, plagued by concern for the tall, silent man she'd just left.

We've unravelled one mystery. I wonder if another will ever be revealed.

———

ON SUNDAY EVENING, AS PROMISED, ED ARRIVED shortly after five o'clock and sat quietly next to Harry in the armchairs, talking about the weather, fish, and a raft of other everyday subjects.

Alice speared the leg of mutton with the fork, and as the pale pink juices ran into the pan, she froze and stared at the back of Ed's head.

Why hasn't he been conscripted? He's fit, healthy, and by all accounts has no reason not to serve his country?

Throughout the meal, Ed appeared to relax as he, Paddy and Harry chatted amicably. All evening, Alice struggled to push her thoughts to the back of her mind and join in the conversation. While she cleared the table and washed and dried the dishes, Ed cheerfully played a board game with the boys, and her amazement —and her impatience—grew.

They had no sooner waved goodbye as he headed out into the dark night than she leaned close to Harry and whispered, "Why hasn't he been called up? He's not in the Home Guard, is he? How come the government haven't chased him?"

Harry rubbed his chin and stared at her. "I don't

know, love. I suppose none of us has thought of it. I mean, most people don't know anything about him, and apart from the locals and the boats that pull in, I don't think he sees anyone?"

"So why haven't one of the skippers reported him?"

Harry shrugged. "Perhaps he's had an exemption for some reason. Lord knows he's private enough, and even he doesn't seem to know his history. Or perhaps those who do know him are like us, love, just trying to run our farms and get on with life."

"Hmm. Well, I still think something is very odd."

"You're probably right, but odd or not, it's none of our business."

Alice had a troubled night, tossing and turning as visions plagued her—those of a tall, blond-haired man who strode across the swamp and into darkness.

She woke tired, lethargic, and with a pounding headache that refused to dissipate.

September arrived with clearer weather, although the temperatures remained cool. With the road now dry enough to travel on, Alice joined Harry in the truck for an excursion into town.

George had returned to the boarding house in Whangarei, and Timmy and John were ensconced behind the walls of Waioneke School, so this journey would involve just her and Harry.

Alice dashed around as if she was twenty again. She washed her collar length hair and let it dry in thick waves while completing her outside chores, then hurried back to their bedroom to dress. Her well-worn but smart, tailored jacket complemented her white blouse and grey skirt, and she pinned the brooch, a sprig of purple heather set in a cluster of tiny green pieces of glass, onto her lapel. Grimacing at the mirror, she tucked the greying curls that had been blonde only a short time ago behind her ear, placed her best winter hat on her head, and secured it with two decorative hatpins.

With a swipe of her one and only lipstick around her mouth, she popped it into her handbag and joined Harry outside. The wind whipped around the shed, and she laughed and clutched her hat. It wasn't going anywhere, but nevertheless, she held it firmly until she reached the open passenger door of the truck.

"My lady." Harry gave a mini-bow and grinned. "A day out, all to ourselves. What a treat?"

"I know. I just hope we don't get bogged, because I haven't got my gumboots with me and I'm definitely not pushing!"

Harry patted her knee as he settled into the driver's seat and pushed the start button. "We'll be fine. I promise we'll have a great day."

The trip seemed to take forever—not because the road was so churned up and muddy, but because everyone in the district appeared to have had the same idea.

While Harry loaded the truck with numerous agricultural supplies, Alice dropped her grocery order into Mr Jones and walked up the hill to the Federated Farmers building where the monthly Women's Division meeting was scheduled to begin.

Although an irregular attendee, Alice was delighted to be greeted by familiar faces and introduced to new ones.

The president, Olive McMaster, sailed towards her with her hair piled on top of her head and her hand firmly grasping the arm of a slightly built woman Alice guessed to be about ten years younger than herself.

"Hello, Alice. Lovely to see you again. I would like you to meet someone who has recently moved out your way." She turned to the younger woman and swept her arm in a gracious mid-air gesture. Alice stifled a giggle and focused on the newcomer. "This is Sylvia Hatton—and, Sylvia, I'd like you to meet Alice Simpson."

She beamed from one to the other as if she had just announced the winner and runner up of an important competition.

"Well then, I'll leave you to get acquainted and go and speak to some of the other ladies."

Alice nodded and smiled at Sylvia, holding out her hand. "Welcome. It's wonderful to meet new people. It gets a bit lonely at times—well, not really lonely, because I have the family and hordes of animals and things to do but, you know, just not many women to talk to …" She trailed off, suddenly aware she was being gushy. If it bothered Sylvia, she didn't show it and clasped Alice's hand in both of hers.

"It's lovely to meet you too, Alice. Shall we sit down over here and get to know one another while we wait for the others?" She pointed to two unoccupied seats arranged in a semi-circle facing the long, narrow trestle table, clearly designated for the committee.

"Let's." Alice walked over and plonked herself in a chair, angled slightly to face Sylvia. "Where are you living?"

"We've just bought a farm near Mairetahi. Do you know that road?"

"Sort of. I haven't been down it, but we pass it on the way to our place."

"Of course. It's a bit rough, and there's no house yet, so we're living in a shed while one is being built—right at the end of the property overlooking the harbour." She clutched her bag as it threatened to slip off her lap and grinned at Alice. "I don't think I've seen another woman to talk to for weeks."

Alice chuckled and glanced over to the table where the committee appeared to be taking their seats. "I understand completely," she whispered.

Sylvia's grey-blue eyes twinkled as her smile lit up her whole face.

Alice returned the smile and tried to concentrate on Olive's welcome speech.

I've met another friend. Perhaps I could invite Sylvia and Irene over for morning tea some time? Her thoughts ran on while the discussion about Land Girls and the war effort faded to a muffled monologue in the background.

CHAPTER 26

Socialising with friends and neighbours took a back seat for the next few weeks as spring arrived with a vengeance, bringing with it an abundance of new lambs.

The daily rounds of hundreds of heavily pregnant ewes brought a heavy workload, but Alice loved it. She never tired of the miracle of birth, even though it went hand in hand with complications and sometimes sorrow.

By the end of October, she had eight lambs in a pen behind the shed to hand-rear, mostly the result of multiple births to mothers who appeared unable to raise more than one. In addition to the extra mouths to feed, Josie produced a pretty little jersey calf and, with more milk than her baby could manage, required hand-milking twice a day. Paddy obliged in the mornings, while Alice organised the boys for school and fed the balance of her menagerie. By evening, she looked forward to her fifteen minutes of peace and quietly leaned against the cow's side while she squirted the milk into the bucket in a steady rhythmic stream.

Daffodils and jonquils flooded the steep slopes below the house. Every year, Alice had divided and replanted the bulbs, and now they covered the small triangle of hillside, enhancing the steadily growing assortment of trees. As passers-by paused for a closer look, Alice swelled with pride. The flowers obviously brought joy, not just to her, but to others.

"Sorry, love. Another one for you." Harry strode towards her as she hung washing on the line. He held a newborn lamb against him, its tightly curled coat still yellow and damp from birth.

"Dare I ask how the mother is?" Alice grimaced.

"She's fine. A set of triplets, and this little fellow is only half the size of the others. Paddy and I managed to get some colostrum from her for him, so hopefully with your tender loving care he'll pull through." He gave her a wry grin as the lamb let out a loud bleat. "See? He agrees with me."

Alice chuckled.

"Put him in the crate in the shed, and I'll tend to him as soon as I've finished here and shifted this cow."

Bonnie, Josie's two-year-old heifer, mooched around the house paddock, eyeing off the washing basket with interest.

"I hope she has a nice calf and is a good milker,

because I don't have time to be making more pyjamas for everyone." Alice shook her head and nodded towards the basket. "I wonder what it is that attracts some cows to want to chew the washing?"

"I don't know, but I think it's time we moved the line into the house yard somewhere."

"Hmm. Now why didn't I think of that?" Alice met Harry's twinkling eyes, and they both laughed out loud.

The subject had been raised after the ravaging of Alice's dress—somehow attracting a younger Bonnie to raise her head and worry the skirt until, by the time Alice went out to bring in the dry laundry, all that remained was a neat bodice with what appeared to be a series of ragged handkerchiefs hanging from the waist-line like a semicircle of flags. It had taken a second chewing of Harry's pyjama pants before Alice's exasperation overflowed and she'd chopped the chewed bits off, hemming the bottoms well above the knee.

"Let me raise the prop for you, and then we can move her into the next paddock," Harry said. "She'll be safe there until a few days before she's due to calve."

Laying the lamb on the grass in the sun, Harry helped Alice hang up the washing before hoisting the line into the air with the aid of a lengthy tea tree stake, forked at the tip. She picked up the lamb, and they ushered Bonnie towards the gate adjoining the next paddock.

"How's Paddy today?" Alice frowned. Her concern for the old man intensified as his arthritis worsened.

He now needed a stick to aid his walking, and she had to bite her tongue when he eased himself into his chair at the dinner table, slowly and with great care.

"Uncomplaining as usual. I'm just hoping he feels better as the warmer weather sets in."

"Do you think we should take him to a doctor?"

"Huh. I doubt he would allow us to take him anywhere near town, never mind into a doctor's surgery or hospital." Harry rubbed his chin. "The best we can do is to keep him warm, well fed, and of course, help him whenever possible."

Alice nodded and waited for Harry to close the gate after the cow. Then she tucked the lamb more firmly under one arm, reached for his hand, and they walked back to the house.

———

FOR THE FIRST TIME SINCE SHE COULD REMEMBER, ALICE struggled to generate enthusiasm as Christmas approached. It wasn't just the difficulty in obtaining the treats and ingredients that spoke of this special time of year, but more the fact that they would be alone. Rationing of fuel meant that travelling to visit family was out of the question, and a despondency seemed to settle over the whole community.

She was sliding a cake into the oven—a plain butter recipe with only a swirl of last year's blackberry jam to enhance it—when Flossie barked. Her tone determined the situation, and this time it was high and excited, announcing the arrival of a visitor she knew.

Alice wiped her hands and tucked a lock of hair behind her ear as she went to the back door.

"Hello. It's only me!" Irene's cheery call lifted Alice's spirits, and she beamed at her friend.

"Come in. I'll put the kettle on."

She bustled about making a pot of tea and setting out her best china cups while they chatted about nothing of importance. Then, settled comfortably in the armchairs while they sipped the hot drink, Irene's chatter took on a serious note, and Alice moved to the edge of her seat.

"I've got a suggestion. With the war and the year we've all had with rain and everything, we've been feeling a bit low, so I thought perhaps we could put on a Christmas get together for the community at the school. What do you think?"

Alice pondered for a minute and opened her mouth to speak, then closed it again as Irene continued.

"I don't know anyone out this way who has family coming to visit, and everyone's busy with shearing and haymaking around Christmas. So I thought we could begin with a small church service and sing some carols, then share lunch, which would consist of everyone bringing contributions. After we've eaten, the children could play cricket or rounders or something while the adults talk and try to make the best of it."

Alice smiled, and a thread of excitement began to

unravel within her. "I think that's a wonderful idea. Shall we have it on Christmas Day itself?"

"I don't see why not. There's still a couple of weeks of school left, so I can ask Maurice if he'll let the children make invitations to take home to their families and hand out to those who are not involved in the school. We could also ask him if he would organise some sports equipment and games for the day, and the men could get there early and erect a couple of big tents and trestle tables for the food—which you and I can coordinate." She stopped and placed her empty cup on the small table beside her then hugged her knees, beaming widely.

"I can see you've given this a lot of thought already."

The next hour passed quickly as the women discussed plans and made a list of delegations. As soon as she had waved goodbye to Irene, Alice sat and wrote to Maud.

Fantail Ridge
South Head
10 December 1941

Dear Maud,

How are you all? I had to write as soon as possible to tell you our good news. In your last letter, you said how disappointed you were that we couldn't get together this Christmas—and I totally agree. However, I've just had a visit from Irene, and we are going to make the best of our isolation and get the community together for Christmas Day.

Like you, I have been feeling a bit low lately. It's not just the war itself, it's the anxiety we all feel not knowing what is going to happen in the world, and of course having such a wet, miserable year weather-wise hasn't helped. I think a celebratory get together will be just what we all need. Perhaps you could consider doing something similar at your end?

I really don't have much other news this week. Timmy is looking forward to going to boarding school with George next year, which has been a surprise to me. After all the fuss he made when he started school, he seems to really enjoy it—although I think the sport and games play a much greater importance than anything academic does!

Because of the rain, our hay is really thick and should be a good crop, but it will be almost February before we can cut and bale it. Both Harry and Paddy have been hobbling around—Paddy with his arthritis giving him so much trouble, and Harry still has times when his leg injury gives pain. No wonder the army politely declined them!

Speaking of the army, I am puzzled as to why Ed wasn't conscripted? I don't think anyone has given it much thought except me (or maybe no one wants to discuss such a touchy topic?). Anyway, we'll invite him to the Christmas function and see if he turns up—perhaps someone might touch on the subject. His reaction could be interesting.

The horses are a godsend to us, and we enjoy working with them as well as riding. With George coming home next *week, however, we really need another one. I don't suppose Dougal knows of a suitable spare horse somewhere? Stormy is only fit for little ones to walk around in circles on now— like us all, age is marching on!*

Almost lunchtime here now, so had better get a move on.

Lots of love to you all,

Alice

Christmas arrived and excitement bubbled at the school grounds. After a week of rain, the day dawned clear and sparkling. Even the sun seemed clearer and more intense than usual, and although cool, the wind abated as over thirty adults and children arrived in various methods of transportation.

From early morning, Alice rushed around preparing food, mixing up bottles of cordial, and pressing her new dress and the boys' shirts. At the same time, Harry and the children joined others at the school grounds, pitching tents and setting out tables and chairs.

At eleven o'clock, they began with a brief church service in the school room. Alice trembled with nerves as she sat down to play the piano for the hymns and Christmas carols. She needn't have worried as her playing was all but drowned out by the singing, such was the enthusiasm of the attendees.

Afterwards, in spite of rationing, a feast was spread out, and Alice marvelled at the variety of options. Clive and his young wife, Jean, had brought a tray of sliced, roasted venison. It was so tender it fell apart and, dressed with the blackberry sauce that Vince proudly produced, was quickly consumed. Temuera, the manager from a station farther out, had arrived at daybreak with one of his workers, and they had dug and laid a hangi. The layers of fish, kumara, and potatoes were hauled out of the hot, earthen oven and transferred onto roasting dishes in the early afternoon. Together with a pig that had been baking over a fire for hours, the tables groaned with food.

Before dessert could be enjoyed, the schoolteacher set up the cricket stumps, and teams were formed amongst much laughter and light-hearted argument.

It wasn't until they were packing up to return home that Alice realised Ed had not arrived. She dismissed the thought ... inviting him had always been a gamble.

After consuming such an array of food all day, no one was particularly interested in eating tea, and following the completion of evening chores, the boys tumbled into bed with the adults following close behind.

It was pitch dark when Alice woke, startled and with a sense of foreboding deep within her. She lay still, puzzled about what had roused her. The house was silent. Somewhere in the distance, the hoot of a morepork was the only outdoor sound. She tiptoed to the window and peered into the inky night. The silhouette of the puriri tree was just visible against the pale light of a new moon, and stars shone clear and bright above.

As the cold seeped through her thin nightgown, she climbed back into bed and pressed against the warmth of Harry's body.

Too much rich food, I suppose.

Eventually, she closed her eyes and drifted off to sleep.

———

"A PENNY FOR THEM."

Alice smiled at Harry's comment. "I'm not sure they're worth it?"

"Come on. You can tell me anything. You know that."

As they followed the cow down the paddock and through the gate, Alice frowned and met Harry's gaze. "I'm not sure why, but I feel something's not right. Ed didn't turn up yesterday and yet I really thought he would—even if only for an hour or so."

"Are you saying you think something is wrong with him?"

"I don't know. I woke in the night, and you know

that's not usual for me. It may have been just a dream, but I felt a sense of anxiety."

"Well, only one thing for it. We'll check on the boys and go down to the wharf. If we take the billy and some smoko, and Ed is mooching about as usual or out in his dingy, we can just wave and pretend we're having a picnic."

"Good idea." Alice grinned and increased her pace.

The boys and Paddy were tinkering in the shed, apparently creating coat hooks from the used horseshoes and bits of timber. Surprisingly, no one wanted to join them, so Alice packed a box with a few sticks, matches, and the necessities for boiling the billy and joined Harry in the cab of the truck.

The sun shone and a gentle breeze blew—just enough to be comfortable. As they pulled into the entrance to the track, a magpie sitting on the fence post raised its head and warbled melodiously, while a tui flew across the track and landed on a flax flower.

Both birds ignored the human intrusion, and Alice turned to Harry. "They're getting quite tame, aren't they?"

Harry shot her a grin as he turned off the engine. "Almost as tame as those little fantails you love so much."

Alice returned his smile and opened her door.

Seagulls shrieked and swirled at the end of the wharf, but otherwise, the shore was as silent as usual.

Alice cast her gaze around the area while Harry called out. "You about, Ed?"

There was silence, and Alice frowned. "Let's go up to his shack and see if he's there. His dingy is tied up, so he can't have gone out fishing."

Harry nodded and led the way along the narrow track towards the camouflaged hut that Ed used as his workshop. He stopped abruptly at the entrance and held his hand up to Alice in a stop sign. "He's here."

She hurried to peer over Harry's shoulder and clapped her hand to her mouth.

Ed was indeed there, lying prostrate on the dirt with a gash across his forehead. Blood had seeped onto the ground, and flies buzzed around the congealed mess.

"He must have had a fall and hit his head on something." Harry placed his fingers against Ed's neck and looked up at Alice. "He's alive. Unconscious though."

First running his hands carefully along Ed's arms and legs, Harry glanced around the shed.

"We're going to have to get him to the house, but he's too big and heavy for us to move."

"He's got a sled somewhere. It's what he used to pull the shearing engine back to our woolshed. I'll have a look." Alice stood and dashed outside.

She ran back to the hut, combing the veranda and outbuildings. Huge stacks of chopped tea tree and driftwood leaned against the back of the building, partially covered with canvas. She lifted the tarpaulin and shuddered as a weta crawled hurriedly away. Then, as she approached the vegetable garden, she saw it—a solidly built timber sled, curved upwards at the front and with a small protective surround made of smooth, grey pieces of wood. It was laden with potatoes, so she lifted the thick, plaited leather strap at the front and heaved it upwards. Her arm muscles quivered, protesting under the unaccustomed weight, until all of a sudden, the load rolled off the back in an avalanche.

She bent her head and breathed heavily as her muscles strained against the heavy load. The empty sled was as much as she could manage, and they would need more help.

"He's very cold, so I think he's been here a while," Harry said.

Alice stared anxiously at her husband. "You stay with him, and I'll drive back home and see if I can raise Vince or Clive on the phone. They're the closest to here, but if neither of them answers, I'll ring Jack and Irene. Someone will be home."

Alice hesitated, waiting for Harry's nod before backtracking as quickly as she could to the truck. Her previous dread of driving it was forgotten as she climbed into the cab and pulled out the start button. The engine coughed into life, and a cloud of exhaust blew back through the open window. She released her breath in a whoosh, plunged the clutch to the floor, and wrestled the gear stick into reverse.

Without stopping to explain to the four startled

faces as she ran past the machinery shed, she continued inside, lifted the receiver, and wound the handle furiously.

Again, she couldn't believe her luck as the operator answered almost immediately.

"South Head three four three please."

The phone clicked and went silent for a few seconds before the ringing began and Vince's friendly tones reverberated down the line. "Good morning."

"Vince, it's me, Alice. I'm afraid something's happened to Ed, and Harry and I can't lift him. Are you able to come and help us please?"

"Where is he?"

"At the wharf."

"On my way. I'll see you shortly."

The phone went dead, and Alice sped back outside, almost crashing into George as he came around the corner. "Is everything alright, Mum?"

"Ed seems to have had some sort of accident and is unconscious. I've rung Vince, and he's coming to help us lift him. We'll bring him here and see what we can do before we make any further decisions."

"Right, I'll come too. You boys stay with Paddy, and we'll be back as soon as we can."

Alice stared at George in amazement as his calm, authoritative voice took over. Her little boy was no longer—he was a teenager and quite clearly had grown into a responsible one at that.

"Come on. Let's go, Mum."

Alice climbed into the driver's seat again, and they roared down the hill in top gear.

Within fifteen minutes, Vince arrived, and between the four of them, they carefully transferred Ed onto the sled and hauled him to the truck. Loading his big frame on the tray was more difficult, but with Alice cradling his head in a towel, they hoisted him up as carefully as they could. Still unconscious, she stared into the pale face and wished, not for the first time, that she had more medical knowledge.

Expecting a doctor to come all the way out here, particularly on Boxing Day, was impossible, and she wasn't at all sure that transporting Ed over the rough road into town was the best idea either.

They transferred him to a bed in the shearer's room, and Alice bathed his injury. The bleeding had stopped, and his breathing appeared normal. Alice observed his increasingly blue forehead and stared helplessly at his limp, otherwise lifeless body. "What can we do?" She shot a worried glance at Harry and he shook his head.

"I'll ring the hospital and see what they advise."

He had been gone only seconds when Ed twitched. Alice's heart leaped as he lifted one arm and brushed his hand across his head, wincing as he did so.

"George. Run and tell Dad he's waking up."

The boy was sitting on the step, periodically glancing at his mother as though trying to read her mind. At Alice's request, he leapt up and shot inside.

Ed blinked and opened his eyes, struggling to sit up, his elbows pressing into the mattress.

Alice lay her hand on his chest. "Hush. Keep still. You're alright now. We're here and are looking after you." She spoke with more reassurance than she felt, willing Harry to return.

Slowly, Ed turned his head carefully as though to absorb his surroundings better. "Alice? Where am I?"

Relief overwhelmed her, and she answered more calmly than she felt. "You're at our place, in the shearer's room. Harry and I found you, and we got Vince and George to help load you on our truck and bring you here. I'm delighted you know who I am after such a nasty bash on the head."

Ed touched his forehead carefully and winced again. He lay his hand back by his side and stared, his expression unchanging, at her.

The light altered as Harry entered the room and stood next to Alice. "Been in the wars, mate. Do you remember what happened?"

For a full minute, Ed said nothing, and Alice was on the verge of suggesting they leave him to rest when he spoke—softly, carefully, and in clear, precise tones. "My name is Edvard Hansen."

Alice blinked and met Harry's gaze.

"Edvard? Do you mean Edward?" she said.

"Edvard. I grew up in Norway."

Suddenly, her intrigue about his accent, the use of *ya* instead of yes, and his huge, strong build all made sense. Her eyes grew wide as her mind raced. "How did you get here? And why here, at South Head?"

He lay in silence for several minutes.

Alice's heart pounded, and she was sure both men would hear it.

Harry propped a pillow behind Ed's head and shoulders, and she bent to hold a glass of water to his lips, tipping it just enough for him to sip.

"Don't hurry. And don't talk if you don't want to," Harry said quietly.

A rumble came from deep within Ed's throat as he began.

CHAPTER 28

Fantail Ridge
South Head
28 December 1941

Dear Maud,

Well, what a lot I have to tell you this week. I hope you all enjoyed Christmas. We had a lovely day at the school, and I could write a whole page describing the food people brought and who came etc. But I have much more interesting news to tell you.

In spite of accepting the invitation to join the Christmas Day celebrations, Ed failed to turn up. So on Boxing Day, Harry and I went to check on him (surreptitiously of course). We got quite a shock to find him injured, unconscious, and on the floor of what he calls his workshop (but it is really a room built like a bird-watching hide that he tinkers in).

Anyway, I had to race home and ring Vince to help us, and we brought him here.

He regained consciousness and, apart from a headache, seems to be healing quite well. He doesn't remember what happened—BUT—he is still here (in the shearer's room) so we can keep an eye on him, and it turns out that the knock on his head has brought his memory back (which we didn't realise he had lost)!

You know how we always thought he was a bit odd—well, he's not. He just couldn't remember anything about his past and presumed he had done something wrong so has tried to hide all these years. His memories are coming back in fits and starts, and he has been pouring his heart out to Harry. He says he grew up in Norway and was a marine engineer and a crew member of a boat that came to Australia and New Zealand, although he can't quite remember why. Anyway, there was discontent amongst the crew (he does remember that bit) and then they were hit by a bad storm and the last thing he recalls about the trip was being washed up on a beach with black sand—our coastline!!

He thinks he must have been the only survivor, and he's a bit hazy about the rest of the crew, but he said the boat was called 'Johanne' and he clung to the lifebuoy, which is probably what saved his life. Apparently, he walked for days and must have crossed the peninsula from west to east, somehow ending up at the wharf where he now lives. Harry had heard rumours that it used to be run by a chap from Yugoslavia, and Ed confirms that now.

He was quite kind to Ed (lonely, I expect) and the two of them got on well for a couple of months. Then the Yugoslav man caught the boat one night, telling Ed he had to do some business in Auckland, and never came back. The groceries he had stored in the shop gradually dwindled away, so Ed made some arrangement with one of the skippers—exchanging fish and shellfish for various staples in order to survive before arrangements were made for Mr Jones to send out groceries (presumably money changed hands?).

He still seems fearful of something, but he and Harry have talked for hours. As soon as he is strong enough (in the next couple of days, I suspect), Harry is taking him to town to speak to the police. I'm not sure what will happen, but I hope they can arrange for him to apply for citizenship here. He says he has no desire to return to Norway.

I asked him how he remembered his name, and he said he didn't! The Yugoslav man had a strong accent, and Ed thought he misunderstood what was said and presumed one of Ed's words was his name. Anyway, he stuck to it. A bit coincidental, but maybe unconsciously Ed recognised something familiar. Who knows?

You can imagine how excited the boys are about it all. The first thing George said was that he can't wait to go back to school to tell his friends!

Hopefully I'll be able to tell you more in a week or two.

Apart from all that excitement, we're glad the weather is clearing up and are hoping to cut the first paddock of hay soon.

Clive and Jean said on Christmas Day that they are going to spend a couple of days with her family in Auckland and are leaving tomorrow, so I'll get them to post this letter for me.

I look forward to your news and will update you on Ed's plight as soon as I can.

Lots of love to you all,

Alice

ED'S RAPID RECOVERY CONTINUED AND, TWO DAYS LATER, he announced he was walking back to his hut. Knowing there was nothing to keep him, Harry convinced him to at least allow him to drive them both into town to sort out his legal status.

The big man glanced down at his ragged shorts and shirt and stared at Harry.

"Perhaps Harry could call into the menswear shop and see if he can buy you a clean shirt and pair of trousers before you go to the police?" Alice said.

Ed ducked his head shyly and nodded. "I will pay you back."

As she waved goodbye to the two of them, Alice crossed her fingers and pressed them against her lips.

Please let the government, or whoever it is, help him.

She pulled her wide-brimmed hat on her head, picked up the digging fork, and followed the lawn around the side of the house to the vegetable garden. Digging the empty bed, she weeded and bashed the lumps of soil with the fork while butterflies completed somersaults inside her and she wished for the day to pass.

———

Innisfree

Kingseat

3 January 1942

DEAR ALICE,

I have just received your newsy letter about Ed. Gosh, what an interesting story. Didn't I tell you there was something strange going on? Poor man. He must have lived a terribly anxious two decades. I can't wait to hear what will happen to him. Will he become a New Zealander? He must be quite smart to have learned English well enough to fool everyone—especially when he lived such a lonely life.

Dougal is on the search for another horse for you. Not quite so easy now as they are in high demand due to the petrol shortage. He has a couple of young ones here that he's bred for hunting so says that he will work on them and sort something out.

I met Mary and Eve last week in Papakura, and we had lunch together. It was really nice—and even nicer to see how busy they have both become and therefore not nearly as critical of us. Actually, I think they rather admire your pluck—I made sure they knew that you drive the truck and car and told them all about Ed. Did I mention that I had also passed on poor Paddy's life story to them a while ago? They didn't say much but hopefully have changed their attitudes towards him.

Catherine has announced she wants to become a nurse when she finishes school. I think she will be a good one as she is so caring. She's growing up fast and is very helpful around the house.

The men are already cutting hay here—hope the fine weather holds or Dougal will be like a bear with a sore head! He does miss being able to have a wee dram of whisky when things go wrong. He disappears into the tool shed a lot, and I suspect some home brewing is occurring.

No more news here. I look forward to hearing how Ed got on!

Love to you all,

Maud

Alice shoved the envelope in her pocket and flicked through the pile of belated Christmas cards and letters before opening and reading each as her heart sank further and further. It seemed that their Irish and English cousins had much more to worry about than New Zealand did—even trying to purchase writing paper was a struggle. Gratitude, appreciation, and a thread of guilt flowed through her. Nestled here on such a beautiful peninsula, the war raging on the other side of the world seemed too far away to be of concern—that is until individual tales of poverty, hardship, and incredible loss filtered into her life.

Even Ed's plight faded into obscurity as visions of bombed cities, towns, and villages played in her mind. Her heart ached as she recalled the bombing of Pearl Harbour only a month earlier. Was the conflict coming closer to their shores? For the first time since war had been declared, fear gripped her.

I need to clear my head.

She kicked off her shoes and pulled on gumboots, grabbed her hat from the hook, and hurried outside.

Flossie followed her as she descended the narrow track into the bush and, step by step, a sense of peace and oblivion to the outside world consumed her. A fantail chittered and swooped in front of her, snatching at the insects raised by her approach. Behind her, Flossie snuffled at the banks and holes in the ground, seeking out rabbits and ignoring her mistress. Alice reached the flat and, reluctant to return to the real world, she turned and backtracked slowly, puffing hard as she pulled herself up the steep, slippery sections.

She hung her hat on the hook and glanced at the clock on her return to the kitchen. If she peeled the vegetables now, she had almost an hour to sit and reply to Maud.

Fantail Ridge
South Head
9 January 1942

Dear Maud,

I received your letter today (thank you) so decided to update you as soon as I could.

Harry had to help Ed complete a number of forms, and they spent hours being interviewed at the courthouse and police station. It seems highly likely that Ed will be granted citizenship, which is a great relief to us all. However, as a citizen—and a fit and healthy one who has not yet reached his fortieth birthday—he will be conscripted and will be required to fight for our country as long as this awful war continues.

Oddly enough, he seems quite happy about this. I think he's grateful to have everything out in the open, and since his accident, has talked more in a week than I have heard him talk in years. As a result, his vocabulary has improved immensely, and even his accent is barely noticeable.

With the new dairy farms starting on the peninsula, and of course the gradual improvements in the road, the cream lorry is now coming out as far as Mairetahi and will bring mail and grocery orders for us. I imagine it won't be long before they divide up some of the big stations out here and more people move into the district.

Meanwhile, we now have the Japanese army to fear. It is reassuring to know the Americans have stepped up their involvement.

I went for a walk through the bush earlier—such a peaceful, beautiful place to visit. It is my solace, and I never stroll through there without being reminded of our joint meander when you last visited. Hopefully we can repeat that very soon.

No more news at this end. Thinking of you all and looking forward to your next letter.

Lots of love as always,
Alice

CHAPTER 29

On the twenty first of February, 1942, the news filtered through that Darwin, Australia had been bombed days earlier. Fear flowed through the community, and New Zealand forces stepped up the security and defence of their tiny country.

A week later, Ed was granted New Zealand citizenship and was promptly conscripted.

Alice invited him to tea the evening before he left, astounded at the transformation in the man as she welcomed him inside. "You look wonderful, Ed. Are you happy?"

"I am, and I can never thank you both enough for the help you have given me."

Alice smiled and waved her arm towards the dining room. "Come in and sit down. Paddy will be here in a minute, and Harry is carving the meat, so it won't be long."

He and Harry sat at opposite ends of the table while John and Paddy took their seats against the wall, and Alice placed the bowl of vegetables on the table. The room seemed full in spite of both George and Timmy being away at school, and Alice glanced at Ed's tall, upright frame. Always strong, his demeanour now seemed somehow commanding as his confidence increased.

The evening passed in pleasant conversation, and two hours later, they stood at the gate to say goodbye.

"Write to us if you can, and I promise we'll write back." Alice smiled and was taken by surprise when he wrapped her in a bear hug. Red-faced, she waited while he shook Harry's hand for an unusually long period then turned and walked away.

"Well, I didn't expect that," Alice whispered.

"He knows that we're the closest thing to family he's got—and he appreciates it."

Alice bit her quivering lip.

It was true, and for some reason, her heart broke at the thought of the years he had lost.

"Come and sit under the puriri tree with me." Harry lay his arm across her shoulders, and together they strolled across the lawn to sit in the fading summer light at the top of the ridge. Alice's park fell away below them, the trees now high and strong and the grass beneath them filled with a palette of tiny white daisies and bright yellow dandelions.

They sat for a long time, silent and holding hands as

the last chirping of birds settling in for the night resonated across the park.

"Did I do the right thing?" Harry spoke softly, and it took Alice a few seconds to register his question.

"In what way?"

"Buying this place. Bringing you here and promising you it would be a good life."

Alice rested her head on his shoulder and gripped his hand tightly. "You did. Life will always have its ups and downs, and war is just a bigger than usual down. But I love it here and will be forever grateful we came. You have fulfilled your promise of making me happy. I am. Very."

EPILOGUE

Fantail Ridge
South Head
10 February 1946

Dear Maud,

How wonderful life is. We are still finding it hard to believe that the war is over—and hopefully we will soon return to some form of normal.

George is ecstatic as he received a letter yesterday from the accountancy firm in Auckland, advising that he got the position he applied for. He will, of course, have to study while he works and will eventually be able to apply to be a member of the New Zealand Society of Accountants. He is to start in two weeks, so we have been rushing around trying to buy him new clothes—not easy with such reduced supplies in the shops. Apparently, we can't expect any improvements there for some years as the world returns to manufacturing items other than those required in a war!

Harry's sister Nancy (remember the sister who's only son, Phillip, went to war and was sadly killed in Europe?) has offered to have George lodge with them. Her husband, Fred, is quite a lot older than her and is not in good health, so I imagine having George staying will help take their minds off Phillip.

Tim (apparently, he is too old to be called Timmy now) is determined to leave school too and has already lined up an apprenticeship with the Kaipara Dairy Company as a mechanic. He has never been particularly interested in studying (his favourite subject is sport!), so Harry and I have reluctantly agreed. It's a shame I had to buy him new shorts for only two weeks, but at least John can wear them.

So—that leaves just John, and I will make the most of his company while he's at home. Our house will be awfully quiet when he goes to boarding school next year. Paddy is still here, and getting frailer. But he's a great help and good company for us both.

Our other news is that we've received a letter from Ed. He's back in New Zealand and has applied for one of the balloted farms that the government are offering—hopefully here on South Head. We dearly hope he gets one as it will be nice to have him home again. Isn't it funny—home?

It doesn't seem that long ago that you and I sat at your kitchen table and talked about me living so far away from our home. Now I realise that it was never really my home. It was our family's community, and I was grateful to be in it, but Harry and my lives are here now, on this beautiful peninsula. Fantail Ridge is our home.

I'm looking forward so much to seeing you all here next weekend. We will have a family picnic on the lawn under the trees—perhaps we could begin a new trend and have a family picnic every year in February when the weather is at its nicest. What do you think?

See you on Saturday.

Love always,

Alice xx

ACKNOWLEDGMENTS

This story was inspired by my maternal grandparents. The choices they made, the stories they passed on and the love they gave, shaped us all. I have taken the liberty of drawing on their oral histories in addition to the opportunities, guidance, and beautiful farm they shared with our family, and used them for my own imaginative purposes.

In the course of writing this book, I have consulted many texts and talked to those who were willing to share their memories and knowledge. A special thank you to ninety-seven year old Lesley Tracey, whose recollections were as sharp today as most peoples are at half her age. I am especially indebted to my sisters, who spent days trawling through family documents, photos, souvenir booklets and keepsakes, each with their own snippets of information. I would like to thank Leigh Bosche from the Helensville Museum for her help in sourcing a copy of *Pioneering Women of South Kaipara* (Helensville and district Historical Society Inc.) and *Men Came Voyaging* (C.M. Sheffield). Special thanks also go to those historians in my family who have shared and documented so well, the numerous generations of our history.

Thank you to Lauren and Anna (CREATINGInk) for your ongoing, much appreciated editing skills, and to Patti Roberts (Paradox Book Covers) for your beautiful book covers, promotional graphics and so much more. Thank you to my friends and family for your honest and appreciated critique, suggestions, and support. I hope I have done you proud. This is for you.

THE LUPIN FIELDS
CHAPTER ONE

September 1966

Dawn Simpson hadn't cried since the day her grandmother was buried, six years earlier, and she certainly would not cry now.

Have I made a huge mistake?

She clasped the letter firmly in her fingers. Butterflies swirled inside her as she and John approached the dwelling—a weatherboard cottage perched in the middle of an empty paddock, stark and forlorn. The wire netting surround, its shiny new posts glistening in the afternoon sun, reminded her of the ugly mesh that imprisoned her old school grounds.

The green Chrysler Valiant hit a bump and she clutched the dashboard, turning to meet her husband's grin and her heart skipped a beat. John's blue eyes crinkled at the corners, the creases fanning into pale lines against his handsome, tanned face while a row of tight curls edged his forehead. She smiled fleetingly and returned her gaze to the building. *This can't be it. We must have to travel farther over the farm yet.*

While he negotiated piles of gravel, she recalled the conversation she and her best friend, Ann, had shared a year ago.

"I'm going to marry a farmer." Ann had been quite adamant, ignoring Dawn's eye roll. "Farmers are wealthy because the government provides subsidies, and the money that wool and meat are bringing are at an all-time high. Plus, they can please themselves what hours they work."

Dawn hadn't argued. She had never visited a farm, or taken any interest in country living, so how would she know if Ann was telling the truth? If Dawn married at all, she'd decided it would be to a man who worked in the city and drove a fine car—someone who would take her on holidays to Australia and cruises to far-off lands. And, of course, be a good father to the horde of children she planned to have.

It's me who's married a farmer, and you're the wife of a builder, so we both got that wrong.

The vehicle slowed and came to a stop, facing the dwelling.

The sturdy timber cottage was exactly like dozens of other New Zealand post-war houses. Its tiny front porch and vacant, staring windows bore no resemblance to what she had envisaged. While the relocated dwelling had been moved to its new destination on

Fantail Ridge, she was spending long hours at the salon basin, shampooing customers' hair and dreaming about her new life. In addition to the new home, her wish for a cat and perhaps a dog would finally be realised, especially as she no longer had to contend with her mother's dislike of animals.

As she stared in dismay, she fidgeted with the envelope. Where was the low-set building with a veranda along the front and French doors opening onto it from every room?

Her glance dropped to the letter. It had been delivered to the Fantail Ridge homestead where John's parents, Harry and Alice, had welcomed them with a delicious lunch, a pile of mail, and boxes of wedding presents. Ann's card was on top and the only one Dawn had opened. It wasn't a gushy wedding card covered with bows and glitter; this was plain white and featured a pair of pretty fantails on the front. Inside, the script was all Ann's—short, sweet, and to the point. Dawn could remember every word.

Dear Dawn,

By the time you get this, you will have returned from your honeymoon and be enjoying the beauty and privacy of your very first home. Congratulations!

I can't wait to hear all about it. Please write soon.

Meanwhile, remember my favourite saying: "There are two types of people in this world. Doers and dreamers. I'm the first and you are the second. So live your dream and share it with me so I can dream with you—or at least, try.

Lots of love to you both,
Ann

PS – Do you like the card? I thought it very appropriate considering you're now living on "Fantail Ridge".

Perhaps she was right. John had been enthusiastic about the purchase. "A perfectly well-maintained house," he'd said. "No longer required —new development on Auckland's outskirts. You don't have to worry about a thing."

In the flurry of excitement, an old, stylish house, filled with character, had filled her mind—something similar to the only home she had ever known.

She inhaled deeply as she stared at the disappointing dwelling. Ugh. What was she going to do? But she already knew. She was going to have to consider herself lucky to have a husband and a place to live.

"This is it. Our new home," John said. He took Dawn's hand and rested it on the leather seat between them. Not a shrub, a tree, or any sign of life near the building. She swung her gaze from the house to her husband and her dismay grew.

"Oh." She bit her lip as her mother's voice resonated in her head. "You said the house was nice—not something the government would provide for the homeless."

Silence filled the car for a few moments as she faced John's apologetic smile. He opened the door and got out slowly, quietly. His hand trailed lightly on the bonnet as he made his way to the passenger side, his eyes fastened on hers. Years of arguments and reaction to her mother's sharp tongue had not served her well, and now she wished she had been taught to look for positives instead of always dwelling on the negatives.

John wrenched the door open and held out his hand. Their love was new and fragile, and the last thing she wanted to do was upset him.

"I'm sorry, darling. You and your parents have done your best. I'm just tired," Dawn said.

"And a bit grumpy?" He gave a wry grin as she swung her long legs out of the vehicle. A gust of wind caught her fair curls, blowing them across her face. She raised a hand to her brow, grateful for the few seconds to bury her head against his shoulder and hide her disappointment.

Am I like my mother? Suppressing the moan that threatened to escape, she stepped back and met John's eyes, willing her own to fill again with hope and fervour. Her chest tightened as something warm unfurled within it. She had promised to have and to hold, for better, for worse, for richer, for poorer … She plastered a smile on her face and reached out. *I must not dampen his infectious enthusiasm.* "Are you going to carry me across the threshold?"

"Of course," he rasped.

For a split second, her legs remained glued to the ground, her eyes resting on the solid, tightly closed door of the cottage. She leaned forward as John swept her into his arms, one work-roughened hand around her back and a strong arm under her knees. After kicking open the ornate wrought-iron gate, he carried her up the path and fumbled with the handle, almost dropping her in the process. Dawn tightened her grip around his neck as they fell through the open doorway. They giggled like school children, her outburst seemingly forgiven, and he set her back on her feet.

"Welcome to your home on Fantail Ridge," John said.

She took a deep breath, tentatively looking around as the last frayed threads of excitement faded to apprehension. Chewing the inside of her cheek, she folded her arms over her chest and rubbed her shoulders.

"It's very cold," she said softly.

"It won't be for long. We'll light the fire, and once we've unpacked, it'll be perfect. The windows let plenty of sun in, and it's small enough to keep cosy and warm." John wrapped her in a tender hug and she leaned against him for a moment, her face pressing against the pulse in his neck. *Life. Live. Love*, his beating heart reminded her.

"That's true." She raised her eyebrows. His excitement was contagious, and she wrestled with her feelings, determined to keep her bluntness under control. It had severely narrowed her field of friends in the past.

"Plenty big enough for us." John released one arm, flinging it in a sweeping gesture and tangling a lock of her shoulder-length hair in his fingers.

"Ouch!" Her hand flew to her head, and his eyes widened in horror.

"Oh, I'm so sorry. I'm such a clumsy twit." He squeezed her against him. "Are you alright?"

She nodded briefly and gazed around the room—if you could call it that. It was more of an enclosed porch. A row of coat hooks adorned the inside wall and a brand new wringer washing machine stood in the corner, nestled against the double concrete laundry tub.

"The laundry?" she asked.

Why hadn't they come through the front door? She hadn't even noticed a front entrance. Consumed with disappointment, she had barely registered the garage and gate that led them to where they now stood.

"Yes, sort of. I suppose it's the room for everything that doesn't have its own space. We'll have the wood box in here over winter, and this cupboard is where the hot water cylinder is." John opened a door to reveal a slim, silver tank surrounded by shelves, and she allowed herself to relax a smidgeon as the warmth emanating from the cupboard wafted around her.

"Plenty of space because it doubles as a linen cupboard." He closed the door again and flung open the one next to it, a little less enthusiastically this time. "Bathroom and toilet."

She nodded, a shadow of a smile hovering around her lips. John grasped her hand again and towed her into the small hallway.

Peering into each room as they passed, she tried hard to be optimistic. In the first, a fixed bench against the inside wall provided seating while a small wooden table squeezed between it and the kitchen sink. *Not a good start.* Her heart sank even further. It certainly wasn't the large country kitchen where she dreamed they would spend most of their indoor time, with newspapers and magazines spread over the table and room for her to bake while their children scattered toys across the floor.

"New electric stove, just for you," John said, enthused, as he pointed to the appliance at the end of the Formica bench, and then to the window. "A great view, don't you think? Plenty of warning if visitors are coming." He laughed and grasped Dawn's hand again, gently guiding her out of the room and back into the hallway.

She glanced into the two small rooms on either side of the hall. *Bedrooms?* Four strides led them to the end of the passage, opening into a cosy lounge with a fireplace on the southern wall. Facing east, a large window provided a multi-layered view across the paddock to the Kaipara Harbour. Beyond its sparkling waters, the mainland spread across the horizon, shadowy and distant.

Dawn fixed her gaze on the panorama. All her life she had been a city girl, and now, in spite of the beauty in front of her, a shiver ran down her spine. Exposed and helpless, she reached out and clutched the heavy maroon curtains hanging on either side of the window, the urge to close them so strong she had to steel herself. Taking a slow, deep breath, she studied the fabric as she forced her hands to drop to her sides. *Shabby, but serviceable. They'll do until I can find something better.*

John touched her arm and turned her to face a small, enclosed front porch leading off the lounge. "I should have brought you through here. You would have got a better first impression. Sorry, love."

She shot him a brief grin and followed his gaze through the second doorway into what was clearly the main bedroom.

"Ours. Doesn't the furniture we chose look good? It was only delivered the day before our wedding, so I left Mum to get it ready and make it welcoming for you," he said.

Dawn nodded, annoyance preventing her smile from reaching her eyes. Studying the plain white cotton bedspread and green eiderdown lying diagonally across the bed, the words stuck in her throat. One thing was certain—no matter how much she and John loved each other, she would be redecorating the house to suit her own tastes. How she would achieve this without offending her mother-in-law would be something she'd worry about later.

ALSO BY HEATHER REYBURN

TULLAGULLA SERIES

The Cedar Tree

The English Oak

The Pepperina Grove

A Tullagulla Christmas

FANTAIL RIDGE SERIES

Peninsula Promises

The Lupin Fields

The Scent of Promise

FEATHERWOOD FALLS SERIES

A Stranger in Featherwood Falls

Secrets in Featherwood Falls

Sparks Fly in Featherwood Falls

Clouds over Featherwood Falls

Coming Home to Featherwood Falls

A Festive Featherwood Falls

OUTBACK SKYE

Letters in Blue

Dust on the Heather

The Crofter's Song